CHURCH FOLK
AIN'T GOT
NO SENSE

ECCENTRICH

CHURCH FOLK AIN'T GOT NO SENSE

TATE PUBLISHING
AND ENTERPRISES, LLC

Church Folk Ain't Got NO Sense
Copyright © 2016 by Eccentrich. All rights reserved.

No part of this publication may be reproduced, stored in a retrieval system or transmitted in any way by any means, electronic, mechanical, photocopy, recording or otherwise without the prior permission of the author except as provided by USA copyright law.

This book is designed to provide accurate and authoritative information with regard to the subject matter covered. This information is given with the understanding that neither the author nor Tate Publishing, LLC is engaged in rendering legal, professional advice. Since the details of your situation are fact dependent, you should additionally seek the services of a competent professional.

The opinions expressed by the author are not necessarily those of Tate Publishing, LLC.

Published by Tate Publishing & Enterprises, LLC
127 E. Trade Center Terrace | Mustang, Oklahoma 73064 USA
1.888.361.9473 | www.tatepublishing.com

Tate Publishing is committed to excellence in the publishing industry. The company reflects the philosophy established by the founders, based on Psalm 68:11,

"The Lord gave the word and great was the company of those who published it."

Book design copyright © 2016 by Tate Publishing, LLC. All rights reserved.
Cover design by Joana Quilantang
Interior design by Shieldon Alcasid

Published in the United States of America

ISBN: 978-1-68254-978-0
1. Religion / Christian Life / Family
2. Religion / Christian Life / Love & Marriage
15.12.16

To Antonio Williams Sr., thank you for showing me the meaning of life through your death.

Prologue

It's so hard being a single pastor. Everybody has their say in what I'm doing and who I'm doing it with. I promise I'm almost one scripture away from throwing in the towel—members lagging, not paying tithes, half coming to church, and they got enough time to tell me how to run my life. On days like this is when I miss you the most, Traci.

At thirty-five, Pastor Daniel Shepherd was widowed after tragically losing his wife in a plane crash on her way back home from visiting her parents who were five states away. He was six foot three, 220 lbs., and coffee-complexion. And although his hair was on the naughty side, he always kept it cut low, and he kept his goatee nice and trimmed. He also had the most beautiful pair of gray eyes and was a man who prided himself on staying healthy and fit because anyone who had ever been to an African American service knew that you had to be in shape because all hell could break loose at anytime and your whole church could be shouting at once. He believed firmly that if God were to use him to lead his people, then he must do his best to practice what he preached and prepare his body as a temple unto the Lord. Even though pastoring was his full-time job, he also owned a dry-cleaning business that did well, and because of this, every single woman in Come Take a Walk by My Side Church of God in Christ was seemingly auditioning to become his wife.

Although he knew that dating and being a pastor were hard enough as it was, he tried his best to not become intimately involved with anyone in his congregation. Normally, this would have been an easy thing to do; however, he had recently, for the past few months, been getting to know Sister Cheryl Gooding more personally while they were working on a church program together. He had not seriously dated anyone since losing his wife nearly one year ago.

But, Lord, I sure do like Sister Gooding. Yeah, sure, she has her shortcomings, but so do I. But overall, she is a very sweet lady, and above all, I believe she sincerely loves me.

All this was going through Pastor Shepherd's mind, as he stepped out his office after counseling a couple on how to respect each other in their marriage. He shouldn't do that because he told them not to get married in the first place.

Now it is six months later and here they are a two-headed dog pulling in different directions; unequally yoked and trying to make it work, but God answers even the "I told you so" prayers.

Though he was very tired, he pulled himself together to do the work of God.

"Sister Lackey, please do come in," he said in a tired tone.

Sister Julia Lackey rose from her seat, and as she did, she mistakenly dropped her purse. As Pastor Shepherd bent to pick it up, Sister Lackey lowered her head and grazed his lips. Now she knew that Pastor Shepherd was a good man and was doing very well even outside of the church. And since he took over the church almost six years ago, she had her eyes on him, but she knew he was a man of God and was extremely devoted to his wife. But now that his wife was out the way, she saw the perfect opportunity to get in where she fit in and find a daddy for her two young children.

Though a man of God, he was still a man. Now here they were, standing eye to eye, face-to-face, lust flowing between the widowed preacher and the single woman. And while everything in Pastor Shepherd's fleshly man was begging him to take her right there in his office, he managed to say, "What can I help you with today?"

Sister Lackey said, "Well, I came to talk to you about controlling my flesh." She then leaned in and tilted her head, and without realizing it, he did the same. And just as their lips were about to meet, Mother Hollister walked in. And when she witnessed the scene, she placed her hand over her dramatic heart and grasped for air.

1

"WHAT IN THE name of the lily of the valley is going on here?" Mother Hollister was staring at Pastor like he was a matador and she was the bull. Her judgmental stares went from Pastor to Sister Lackey then from Sister Lackey back to Pastor. Choosing to ignore Mother's question completely and refusing to play into her dramatics, Pastor Shepherd calmly asked, "Mother Hollister, how can I help you?"

"Well, I was coming to ask you a question about the upcoming end-of-the-year New Year's Day program, but I see that praise is the last thing on your mind. And as for you, being a lady is more than just being born with a—"

"Now hold on just a minute, old lady. You don't know me or what's going on here, so before you judge me, make sure God ain't judging you."

"Pastor, maybe we should just continue this counseling session another time. Thank you anyways." And with that, Sister Lackey all but broke her hips, exiting the pastor's chambers.

"Mother Hollister, I would appreciate it if you knocked before entering my office next time," Pastor Shepherd said.

"Well, isn't it a good thing that I didn't because Lord only knows what would have happened her today on this holy ground. Obviously, God saw fit for me to stop the devil in his tracks and to keep his Word."

"The only thing you stopped was a woman struggling with her Christianity from getting a breakthrough. Now what is it about the program you wanted to discuss?" As far as Daniel Shepherd was concerned, he had just finished listening to twenty minutes of the mother of his church whine and bicker about how she was placed in the end of the program and not the beginning. Go figure. His head was about to explode because if he had to baby one more so-called spiritually mature member of his church, he would just pop.

It was 4:00 p.m., and he had yet to make it home from Sunday morning service. *I wonder what Cheryl is doing*, Daniel thought, as he let what Mother Hollister was saying go in one ear and straight out the other. It had been almost three weeks since he and Cheryl Gooding had conversed on a more intimate level. He needed more time to get to know her because Lord knows he wanted desperately to be married. He not only wanted to be married to be an example to his members by showing that God moved in the lives of his children if they put him first but also he wanted a wife so that he could be a man freely and without the condemnation of the spirit of God.

"I will speak to the event coordinator as soon as I get a chance. Is there anything else you wanted to discuss?"

After thinking for a brief second, Mother Hollister simply stated, "No, I think I'll be going now. And remember, Pastor, you might want to behave yourself!"

"God bless you, and I'll see you Wednesday night at Bible study, Mother." Daniel shut the lights off in his office and closed the door, as he followed Mother Hollister to her car, all the while thinking why on earth anybody would want to be a pastor.

2

CHERYL GOODING GREW up in one of the roughest parts of Michigan, an area known as Flint. She had overcome being verbally, mentally, and physically abused by her mother simply because of who her father was, even though she was the one who chose to let him father her child. For a long time, she held a lot of hatred and animosity toward her mother, an act which hindered her growth in Christ. So before her mother passed away about a year ago, she made it her job to openly forgive her and led her mother to the love of Jesus Christ right before she died from HIV/AIDS from years of sharing needles to feed her heroin addiction. Cheryl also found her father and made peace with his not being there for her, and now they have a wonderful and healthy father-and-daughter relationship, and that she would be eternally grateful to God for.

As Cheryl pulled into her driveway, she reflected on the sermon today. It was truly what she needed. And as much as she would love to speak with Daniel about what she was going through, she knew that it would be hard for the both of them with their newfound attraction and ever-evolving relationship. She had missed Daniel these last few weeks, but she had known that he was busy and decided to wait till he gave her a call. She still couldn't believe that someone of his caliber was interested in her. I mean, she was not a bad-looking woman by any means, but she sometimes felt really insecure when in his presence.

She looked herself over in the mirror, and at thirty-one, she could easily pass for twenty-six. She had mocha-brown skin, almond-shaped hazel eyes, shoulder-length jet-black hair, a thickness that any man would love, and held a master's degree from Michigan State University. But she wondered, if things went any further, would she have the wisdom to be his wife and the first lady of his church?

Cheryl slipped out of her shoes and started to prepare her dinner. She was going to be cooking herself some yellow rice, neck bones, candy yams, mashed potatoes, macaroni and cheese, and some cornbread to top it off. As soon as she got done with her last dish, her phone rang.

"I wonder who this could be," she said to herself. "Hello."

"Hello," a male's voice on the other end of the line stated. Cheryl's lips instantly spread into a smile, and she had to compose her joy, gather her senses, and state in a calm, cool, and collected voice.

"Hello, Daniel, how are you? You were just on my mind."

Hiding his own composure, he said to her, "That's an awesome thing, because you were on my mind as well, hence the phone call. You left in a hurry today after service, so I wanted to make sure everything was okay with you."

Listening on the other end of the phone, Cheryl was a bit disappointed, but she managed to say, "I am doing well, thank you for calling. But is that the only reason you were calling?"

Internally asking himself if he should state the fact that he also loved the sound of her voice, he finally concluded that he would.

"Yes, but I also needed to hear your voice."

"Well, in that case, I was just preparing dinner. Would you like to come over in, say, an hour or two and join me?"

He was elated by her invitation and answered with all sincerity, "Of course, I would love to."

WHY IN THE name of the lily of the lowest valley is Pastor Shepherd carrying on like a heathen, Mother Hollister thought, as she pushed her way through the large heavy oak door that was about as old as she. She entered her home and threw her purse on the floor and paced about her original hardwood floors with a thud.

"In a time such as this, I need my prayer warrior," she said aloud, as she began walking to the phone. You see, she called upon the other mother in the church and one of her oldest friends whenever she needed help *praying*, however, strangely, this was only when the topic at hand burned her very lips, in anticipation of being told. She sat down harshly in her favorite chair and began dialing the numbers to her friend Mother Mason's house. The phone was not good and on its second ring when she began to grow impatient. "Where on earth are you," she shouted into the empty line. On the fourth ring, her friend answered, "The Mason residence, how can I help you?"

"Mae-lee, what in the John Brown took you so long to answer the phone," Mother Hollister yelled, as she let out a sigh of relief.

"Well, hey, Bertha Hollister. By the sound of your voice, I reckon you got something for me. By the volume, I'd say it was something big."

See, they knew each other. They had been playing this game long enough to know when the other needed to be lifted up in *prayer*.

See, the two mothers met at the tender age of twenty when the church first opened its doors and had not been separated since. They had watched the church undergo change after change, preacher after preacher, and scandal after scandal. So in their eyes, they owned the church and were merely allowing Pastor Shepherd to rent it out for a while because experience told them he wouldn't be here long, especially after what she saw today. "Well," Mae-lee shouted.

"Girl, we need to pray cause like the good book says where two or three is joined in his name, some good stuff gone happen, and hallelujah. Anyways, girl, today, as I was going to see Pastor Shepherd to discuss the problems with the end-of-the-year program, something in my sanctified spirit told me not to knock. So being the woman of God that I am, I listened and stopped Pastor Shepherd and that little hussy with all 'em kids about to kiss right in the house of the Lord."

"O hell, I mean, oh no, they didn't, girl. The devil ain't got no manners. He so messy, glad you yielded to the Spirit and did God's work."

They continued to talk for hours about the who, what, and when that were going on in the church. And after exhausting all they could possibly talk about, they ended the phone call in unison as they always do. "And until next time, make sure you stay in prayer." See, maybe things would be okay if their conversations could stay between the two of them. But because they always managed to spread gossip, like their waistlines, nothing could ever stay civilized. And sadly, they didn't see it that way. To them, they were simply gathering soldiers for the army of the Lord.

4

"So, Cheryl, please do me the honor of telling me a little bit more about yourself—where you come from, what was your childhood like, what led you to Christ." This was the moment Sheryl knew would come but dreaded nonetheless. Should she tell him everything about her past? Should she trust him with her dark secret? One of which she knew could run him away forever because a man such as him could not love someone with the information she was holding inside.

After racking her brain, she concluded that she would not tell him everything but simply enough to feed his interest. "Well, I grew up in Flint, Michigan. I was my mother and father's only child, so as you could imagine, I was a tad bit rotten. We never had a lot of money, but Daddy had a decent job, and for that time, we were doing well." Sheryl thought over the good times in her childhood and smiled at the memories. "We were doing wonderfully—well, that is until Daddy left. See, my father, Mr. Robert Gooding, decided one morning that my mother was too old and dull for him. So he went out and found himself someone younger and more adventurous. And one morning, when I was seven years old, he left for work and never returned. That was when things took a U-turn and headed the other way." She looked up at Daniel and asked, "More?"

And he answered with all sincerity, "Please that is, if you don't mind."

Sensing a bit of hesitation on her end, he decided to tell her a little bit more about him, in hopes that she would continue to be open with him because his spirit was discerning that she had a secret to tell. And before he got too seriously involved with her, he needed to know what it was because matters of the heart ran deep, and he knew that sometimes the things you opened your heart up to were the very things that could have you running for your life.

"I'll let you take a break and tell you a little bit more about me. Well, I grew up in Rochester New York, and at a young age, I was exposed to the miracles of Christ. However, I was also exposed to the tricks of the enemy. You see, my father was a preacher, and he ran the church I grew up in, Chapel of Deliverance. And of course, this is where he met my mother. I remember on Sunday mornings, I would wake up to the sweet smell of homemade pancakes made from Jiffy Mix and maple syrup. We would sit at the table, say our grace, and eat as a family before we went to church every Sunday before service.

"However, as with any family, we had our problems. My father was an alcoholic, and he used to beat my mother. I remember walking in from school, and my daddy had been drinking. That was the first time I saw my dad beat my mother like a dog on the street, but unfortunately, it would not be my last. I remember one day he told my mother he would beat her to sleep. And one day, he beat her, and ironically, she never woke up. That was the day, at the age of ten, that I started running from Christ, even though at the tender age of four, I felt the calling he had for me. And as you can see, God has a way of finding you no matter where you may go. Anyways, I just couldn't understand how Daddy could go to church during the day then at night drink and beat on my momma. I loved my mother, she was everything to me and Daddy. Well, Daddy is in jail serving out his sentence, and I have not spoken to him since the night he killed my mother. That was eighteen years ago."

Cheryl was looking at Daniel, and her heart went out to him. Staring at him, she saw so many different emotions that she, for a brief moment, realized he was human, and this gave her hope.

After digging up emotions that neither had allowed themselves to feel in years, an awkward silence fell over them. As they sat and finished eating dinner, Daniel wondered where their relationship would lead. He did know that he had a sincere interest in Cheryl, and he believed that she had one in him as well. However, he could not help but notice something in her eyes, like she was hiding something, and he wondered why she would not tell him. Internally, he hoped that whatever she had buried in her past would not determine their future. In the midst of his thinking, Cheryl interrupted his train of thought to ask, "So, Daniel, how did you enjoy dinner?"

He answered honestly, "Well, if I knew that you could throw down like that, Ms. Gooding, I would have snatched you up a long time ago."

And she replied in a flirtatious tone, "Well, better late than never."

After talking and laughing for a few more hours, Daniel stood up to leave. And without even trying or noticing, he drove Cheryl over the edge and her body to new arenas. As he smiled and showed her his pearly whites, beautiful dimples, and banging body, she thought, *Now, Lord, why did you have to make him so fine because the devil is playing hardball right now.*

"Well, Cheryl, I must get going. I have a lot of work to do. But I truly enjoyed this time we've spent today," Daniel stated, as he gently caressed Cheryl's arm and made his way to the door. *Lord, thy God, this woman's skin is soft as satin. And is it my mind, or does her skin smell of strawberries? Lord, I better go because I ain't touch or smelt a woman since my wife died.*

"I enjoyed you as well. I hope we can do this again of course, without the long break in between."

Pastor Shepherd opened the door, but something was keeping him from crossing over the threshold. It was sort of hypnotic, something sort of luring God. It had him yearning to be touched. And before he could talk himself out of it, he turned around, grabbed Cheryl's waist, and gently placed his lips on hers with hopes that she would not reject him. Regrettably, she broke their bond and lowered her head to the ground.

Daniel then placed his hand underneath her chin and gingerly brought her face to his. And looking profoundly into her eyes, he asked her, "Cheryl, what is it?" As she pondered her next move, she again lowered her head in what Daniel thought was fear but was really shame. However, Daniel again returned her face to his and demanded in a low sinuous tone, "Please, look at me, beautiful." After such an invitation, how could she deny him? So she complied and answered, "Daniel, this is wrong. I don't feel like this is appropriate for a man—"

"A man in what? My position? Cheryl, I am a man of God, true enough, but I wrestle with the same temptations as anybody else. And all I want right now is to caress you with my lips. Is that too much to ask?"

Before she could answer, he wrapped his masculine arms around the small of her back and again placed his lips on hers. But this time, she conceded in defeat and rescued his lips from falling with hers. He held on to her cheek as he kissed her ever so gently. And as she tiptoed to meet his passion, an electric current formed between the two of them, and Daniel parted her lips with his tongue to savor her presence. You see, he wanted to leave her home with her aroma and leave her with his. As they kissed deeper, he began to caress her backside, one that he marveled just how well it was put together. And Cheryl was making her way to the bulge that was forming in his pants, one that looked very promising. But just as she was about to undo his belt buckle, he pulled back. Daniel tried with force to regain control of his emotions because he knew emotional decisions usually meant bad decisions.

"Lord, Jesus, the true and living vine. Cheryl, sweetie, I think you were right. I think I should be going."

"Um, okay, yea, maybe that's the best thing to do before we do something we regret."

"I ain't say nothing about regretting. It's just that I have to be the first partaker of the gospel. I thought I would be able to handle the kiss, but it has been a while, and you, you feel so wonderful. However, if I am to lead people into the kingdom of God, I have to yield to the Holy Spirit, and I hear him clearly. This is neither the time nor the place, but please don't think for one second. I think that I will regret the experience and just keep being you, and I guarantee that I won't disappoint either." And with that, he walked out of her home. And as he left, he had no doubt in his mind that he could make good on that promise, and she had no doubt in her mind that before all this was over, she would be head over heels in love with a pastor. And again, her spirits diluted, as she knew one day, she would have to tell him the truth.

5

QUINCY TILT WAS Pastor Shepherd's most trusted deacon and best friend. See, Deacon Tilt and Daniel had been friends since way back when Moses parted the Red Sea. While not as handsome as Daniel, he was by no means shabby. He was five foot eleven, chocolate skinned, well-defined, and had some of the most tempting lips you would ever see. And like Daniel, he was a successful black businessman. He was married to Samantha Tilt and the father of a three-year-old beautiful little girl named Cadence. And after many attempts, Sam had finally conceived and was now pregnant with her first child. When Cadence was just five months old, when her mother walked out on her only child in order to live the life she no longer felt she could have with a child, from that day, Quincy was thrown into fatherhood but knew he had to put aside his demons and be there for his daughter.

Though he and Daniel were tight, he didn't join the church until three years after Daniel took over the ministry. And before he met Samantha, he loved women and made sure he made them pay for what Cadence's mother did.

Quincy first laid eyes on his wife when she and her father first attended the church after moving into town. To him, she had looked like Christmas Day, and from that moment, he pursued her through his pain. However, Quincy's reputation beat him to her, and she refused to become another one of his pawns in his drawer. See, of course, the women of the church had to put Samantha on game that he was a man whore and cared for no one but himself. So when Quincy approached her, she had on the whole armor of God.

As soon as he approached her, she let him know that she knew all about him and had no time for games. But little did she know, Quincy earnestly had an interest in her though he knew nothing about her. Something in him knew that she was the woman he would spend the rest of his life with. And because of that, he was extremely patient with her.

As their relationship progressed, so did hers with his little girl. And from day one, she never treated her like anything but her own, and for that, she would always have Quincy's love.

Pastor Shepherd had watched his friend misuse women because of the error of one, and although he could sympathize, he prayed for his friend and was extremely elated when his friend came back to Christ and into his ministry. After faithfully serving God for a year and being Daniel's armor-bearer, Quincy was appointed deacon. He also still served Daniel and was his right-hand man.

Standing as only a true friend would, Quincy had been there unwaveringly for Daniel when his wife, Traci, died. He handled his business affairs, appointments, bills, food, and anything else that he needed, all the while juggling his own life. And for that, he will always be Daniel's heart and soul.

While Quincy—or Q, as folk call him—earnestly sought God, his shortcoming was women, and he was still fighting the spirits from Melissa, Cadence's mother. As wonderful as Samantha was, he had to stay hidden behind the cross to appreciate what they had because, after all, she was his wife and couldn't just leave. This was what Quincy told himself and was still telling himself since the day his wife told him she was pregnant with their child. Despite the fact that he knew this was supposed to be a joyous occasion, he couldn't shake the truth that since he found out, he'd been having nightmares about her walking out on them, and he would have to talk to his wife about his fears because it was causing him to neglect her so far during her pregnancy out of the fear that she would leave him, just as Melissa did.

What sickened him is that somewhere deep in his conscience he could understand why Melissa was afraid. They were both young and knew nothing about being parents. But was that acceptable? After all, he had stayed. And more so than anything, what kind of woman leaves her child? Perhaps the biggest mystery and thing that bothered him the most was that he did not understand how he could still care about Melissa after she had broken his trust the way she did. He was struggling—struggling with the truth, struggling with his present, but most importantly, struggling with the questions. How could he tell his wife any of this? How could he make her understand? How could he be honest with her without her feeling the way he was feeling now, abandoned?

Now in his defense, before Sam's pregnancy, he had discussed the fears he had with her before about being abandoned but had not told her that they had come to life. He has not been honest with her about this fear being the reason he, up until this point, had not been to a single appointment, rubbed her feet, or, for that matter, had not made any real indication that he was happy she was carrying his child. He loved his wife dearly, that he knew, and he would rather have her than lose her because she felt trapped with two children and a husband.

Before he entered the sanctuary, he said a prayer in order to calm his spirits from the thoughts that were invading him at that very moment. "Lord, I love my wife, and my prayer is that you allow me to love her as you have loved the church and give me the peace and wisdom to know that you have control over everything. Please give me the peace to know that my marriage is blessed. Give me the power to forgive so that I can find peace and be forgiven. Above all, today, Father, I send a special prayer for my boy Daniel. Use him as a vessel, and let him stay focused on you and not on people, amen."

6

As he entered the sanctuary, Pastor Shepherd heard whispering and snickering among his members. As he stepped into the pulpit, he wondered what was going on. If he knew one thing, he knew that he could count on Deacon Tilt to have his back about the things he missed in his ministry. With this knowledge, he tapped Quincy on the shoulder, leaned over, and asked, "Man, what's all the chatter about?"

Quincy leaned over to his friend and whispered in his ear, "Man, where have you been? I have been trying to call you all morning. Man, news about you and Sister Lackey is all over the church. What in the world happened between the two of you?"

Pastor Shepherd answered as calmly as possible, "Man, nothing happened. The lady was making a move on me, and Mother comes barging in my office. I guarantee she is behind this. Q, what if Cheryl hears about this?"

"You like her that much, huh, brah?"

"Yes, and she is already fighting what's happening between us, and because of that, I need no setbacks."

"Jesus Will Work It Out" was being sung in the background, as Daniel closed his eyes and silently sent a prayer for strength and patience. When Daniel walked into the house of worship, he had a word prepared; however, the Holy Spirit just sent him in a different direction, and in spite of that, he was determined to listen to the voice of God. He stood with his shoulders squared, chin up, and eyes focused on doing the will of God, and he started his sermon.

"When I pulled into the parking lot, I had my sermon laid out—what I would say, how I would say it, what book I would be coming from. But as I sat in the pulpit, God led me another way. Before we begin, let's bow our heads. Lord, use me as a willing vessel, let your light shine through me, and I pray that I decrease so that you may increase. In the name of your Son, amen." His amen was followed by several amens and hallelujahs from his congregation.

Before Daniel said another word, he glanced around his sheep. And before him sat gum chewers, chip eaters, texters, liars, cheaters, non-tithe payers, fornicators, and many other things, and these were the people condemning him. But one thing his father used to say that he knew to be true was that heaven would be made up of exes; all of us, by the time we see Christ, would, in fact, be an ex of something that was contrary to the Word of God. However uncomfortable, it was his job to see past faults and look into the heart of people and bring the truth regardless of the circumstances. Daniel preached a word so powerful, so moving that there wasn't a dry eye in the house.

"In conclusion, remember that before you point a finger, remember that there's two pointing back at you. Before you attempt to clear the plank out of your fellow man's eye, please be sure you grab the log out of yours. I stand before you and pose a challenge to you: let he who is without sin cast the first stone. I stand before you a statue of imperfection, but through the love of God, I strive for perfection."

"Yes, Lord," a member yelled out. "Tell it, Pastor," another said, as Daniel wiped sweat from his face and took a sip of water.

"Today, I open the invitation of the altar to you. For those who are broken, for those who are carrying the weight of their sins on their shoulder, for those of you who are buried by your secrets," he said, looking at Cheryl. "I urge you to come to God and give it to him."

The praise team entered the stage and sang so melodic, so peacefully, "So come lay down the burdens you have carried, for in his sanctuary, God is here."

"Come now, the time is now and please know that I will take the first step with you toward perfection, as I am the first partaker of the bread of life. Come for forgiveness and to be forgiving, but most importantly, come to the altar for love."

Almost simultaneously, as on cue in her weekly fashion, Mother Mason and Mother Hollister burst out into the isle shouting and praising God for being such a good soldier in his army. Quincy and Pastor led those in need to the altar and those who didn't recognize the need there as well. And afterwards, Pastor Shepherd felt alive and free, which was quite contrary to what he was feeling just twenty-eight minutes and nine seconds ago before he began his sermon. And he inwardly hoped that this feeling of love and liberation lasted the rest of this Sunday here at his church. But then again, that's what God will do for you. He gives you peace that surpasses all understanding.

And he said to himself, "And that's what church folk will do, try to steal that very same peace."

7

Daniel and Quincy were standing at the door, shaking hands and thanking everyone for choosing to fellowship with Church Of The Lord God when it was clear that they could have been somewhere else. However, with everything that went on today, Daniel would not be surprised if they did not come back. Breaking from his thoughts of church, he looked over at his friend and smiled simply because while he was on the left side, Daniel was on the right side of the aisle. And so it is in the spirit, so shall it be in the natural because Q was Daniel's right-hand man, and if he had anything to do with it, he will always be.

"Well, hey there, Deacon Tilt, how might you be today?"

"I am all right, Ms. Lackey. How are you and the kids?"

"Good, you're too sweet for asking."

Pastor Shepherd couldn't help but notice the way she held on to his friend's hand and couldn't believe the audacity of this woman. *Not only was all this chaos caused by her, but also then she completely dismisses the fact that I am even standing here and throws herself as a married man. I tell you people have no respect for God's chosen ones. And because of this, as the pastor of this house, unfortunately, he is going to have to put this woman in check and do it soon before she singlehandedly brings down God's house—can we say Sodom and Gomorrah.*

"Ms. Lackey, I am going to need to see you in my office before you leave today."

"Yes, Pastor," she said in aggravation then averted her attention back to Quincy, who was talking to another member. "Excuse me. So, Quincy, you know how important fathers are. So do you think you would be able to come over and spend some time with the boys, you know for *spiritual* guidance?" Just as Quincy was about to answer, Samantha walked up behind and cleared her throat, placed her hands on her hip, and stated as calmly as she could, "No, Quincy doesn't make house calls, and if I catch you with your skanky hands on my husband again, you gonna have a serious problem. Q, I'm hungry and ready to go! Daniel, you already know. I am gonna need a call later because we have to talk."

With that, Quincy looked at Daniel and shook his friend's hand and promised to give him a call to make sure he made it home all right, since he had to meet with Ms. Lackey, and she was clearly cut throat.

"Lord, help me because my members have clearly lost their minds. Now I would have to scold Sam for her actions." He prayed although he was clearly thinking that her actions were only right. After a few more members, he closed and locked the doors to his church and appreciatively looked over the sanctuary and silently thanked God because hearing well done thy good and faithful servant will be far more rewarding than quitting now and just running his business or was it?

"Come on in, Sister Lackey, now you don't strike me as the type to beat around the bush. So let me be the first to say that your actions the other day in my office and today with Deacon Tilt were extremely inappropriate. Furthermore, you cannot go around the house of God throwing yourself at every man you come in contact with. I do, however, understand your urgency because of the children, but you must learn to wait on God and allow him to send you a husband. Now the Bible says that he that finds a wife, finds a good thing."

"Oh, please, spare me that religious bull."

"Now hold on, miss, you will watch your mouth, if not, you can simply leave my office."

"It's people like you, people like you who think they are better than me, but let me tell you something. None of you are better than me, and it's about time you knew it. Now I tried to get you—no wife, no kids—but your refused. And why? Because of that lame Jane Cheryl? So if you won't take the bait, I know someone who will, and that's your little friend Quincy. Yeah, I heard all about him, and I am just what he needs to get his swag back."

"Ms. Lackey, we must try to get to the root of your anger, and once we are there, we must dig it up and plant seeds of love and integrity and ask God to instill in you the heart of a woman. I know that this is surly a force of the devil, and I want you to know that there is nothing you can do to stop me from praying for you. You see, I have the love of God in my soul, and that love spills over unto you."

As those words rolled off his lips, Sister Lackey got so close to his face that he could smell the mint-flavored Altoid she had been using to sweeten up her breath. "Let me tell you something Daniel. You don't know everything about what goes on in this church. You don't know the half of what I have gone through with these kids, and if I gotta take someone else's good thing, then so be it."

Daniel grabbed Sister Lackey by the arms and just looked at her. What he saw was a desperate, lonely, misguided woman who, like so many, had been viciously hurt by the very men they sought love from. It was at that moment his anger turned into compassion, and he silently asked the Lord for guidance. Although he knew God would answer, this was not expected or was he prepared for what God had instructed him to do. This couldn't be right. *I mean what if someone walks in? What would they think, Lord? That's all I need for someone to misinterpret this.* Going back and forth for a moment, Pastor Shepherd sighed, sucked in his breath, swallowed his pride, and with all uncertainty slid his hands from her arms and pulled her into his bosom and embraced her.

Though he could feel her resistance, he continued to embrace this single mother, struggling not only in her life, but also in her Christianity as well. Pastor Shepherd embraced her for her children, embraced her for her strength she was unaware of, embraced her for years of hurt, but most importantly, he embraced her with the love of Christ.

Sister Lackey was completely disgusted by this action because just a few moments prior, Pastor Shepherd had been looking at her with such rage. *What does he think he is doing?* If he thought this desperate attempt at a truce would be accepted, then surely he had another thing coming. However, something in her calmed her spirit, and she could not deny that he exuded the love of Christ; and this melted her heart. Sister Lackey unwillingly allowed herself to rest on Pastor Shepherd's chest, and it was there that she cried, and he permitted her to do so. It was in the middle of his strong body that she cried all the hurt the way, where she cried all the things her children saw and the things she had done in her life. It was in his arms that she cried the past away and stepped into the future.

Sister Lackey closed her eyes, thought, and smiled, saying to herself that in his arms was where she sincerely found Christ, and she knew her life would never be the same.

After what felt like hours, she looked up at her pastor, who now stared at her lovingly and said, "I didn't know how much I needed that. I simply didn't know how much I needed Christ." For just a second longer there, they both stood amazed that she had found peace and forgiveness with just one simple gesture. See, it wasn't only the encirclement. It was the fact that in ten years, no man held her without a motive, and she admired Daniel for that. Now they sat and chatted a little more about life, her childhood, among other things, and this time, it was he, Daniel, who admired her strength.

Suddenly, they heard steady yet angry footsteps rapidly approaching Daniel's office. They looked at each other then at the door and bang! The knock on the door was as if someone was pounding into it with a hammer. It was this knock that startled them both causing them to jump from their chairs in fear since Daniel thought his church was empty. They stood side by side waiting and in barged Cheryl. She was bewildered, eyes swollen, head down, and when she looked up and saw her man with the hussy, she flipped. After all, how could he have such a beautiful time with her and now stand so closely to the heffa who was causing all this drama.

"So this is what you want, Daniel?" Cheryl entered angrily, slamming the door behind her. "I sho ain't know you was an actor because you had me fooled. I mean who would've known that you were lying up with this jezebel. Oh yea, Mother Hollister told me all about what she saw."

Daniel stood in awe not believing his eyes. *This could not be the woman who, just a week before, stood before him with such grace and beauty*, he said to himself. Shaking himself back to reality, he remembered that Julia had been in the room to hear all the hurtful and unwarranted words. He turned to her apologetically, looked at Sister Lackey, and he began to understand even more that emotions ruined the soul and carried it out in the flesh.

Cheryl's mouth broke him from his thoughts. "And let me tell you summin', you lil—"

"Now, Cheryl, that is enough. You are completely out of line, and I will not ask you more than once to lower your voice and compose yourself. Sister Lackey, I do sincerely apologize for Sister Gooding's' behavior."

"There is no need for you to apologize. I understand what I have been and viewed as to so many, and that will be my cross to bear for a while. But why start caring what people think about me now. Besides, I would be scared of losing you too. Well, Cheryl, this was really fun, and, Pastor Shepherd, thank you so much." With that, Julia sashayed past what could have been her first lady, with her chest out, hips swaying, shot her a unit, and rolled her eyes because after all, the Lord was not through with her yet. Before she could exit the door, she heard Daniel's voice. "Remember that there is never a reason to get out of character," he said to Julia but looking directly at Cheryl.

Upon Sister Lackey's exit, Cheryl realized she was alone with the man she loved. Cheryl and Daniel stood awkwardly in his office with nothing but air and unspoken tragedy between them. Cheryl was the first to speak. "Daniel, I'm so sorry. I don't know what got into me and can't begin to explain my actions. I have never acted this way before about a man, and because of that, I just don't think we should see each other anymore." There it was again—the past. In her words, he heard it; in her face, he saw it, but he couldn't for the life of him began to make her understand how much he wished she would tell him what he could see all over her face.

"Cheryl."

"Daniel, please don't. Obviously, I am not what you want, and unfortunately, I can't allow myself to be what you want. I'm sorry."

This was all he heard before the footsteps that were once angry, were now apologetic and apprehensive running down the hall and maybe out of his life.

8

THROWING HER KEYS on the table, out of frustration, was Samantha. She couldn't help but feel the distance between her husband and herself, and the reason for that, she didn't know. So instead of probing, which would lead to an argument, she took her daughter and waddled to her daughter's bedroom to change her clothes. Burdened, she sighed and entered the room and closed the door without a single word to her handsome husband, and he said not one word to his wife.

Though Quincy sincerely was troubled by the fact that he seemed to be shunning his wife, he could not control that emotion for some reason. However, he knew that if he didn't, he would lose the best thing that ever happened to him and his daughter. How could he treat the woman who picked him up and nursed him back to health after Melissa left him in a trail of dirt? How could he mistreat the woman who asked no questions but instead accepted his daughter and loved her as her own? He asked himself these questions, but instead of answers, they only led him to more questions. Is it that deep down inside, he still loved

Melissa? Is it that he really feared abandonment? Truthfully speaking, he just didn't know, and because of this, he turned to God. "Lord, whatever it may be, I beg of you to either remove or reveal it so that I can love my wife, as you have loved the church, without condition or emotion."

Meanwhile, Samantha sat with her daughter playing with her dolls. As she sat and braided Barbie's hair, her eyes filled with tears, her heart filled with terror, and her mind filled with thoughts of the man she loved, who physically was right behind the white wooden door but emotionally was a mile away. Sam didn't know if it was her hormones, but she felt a presentiment of nausea, and in the pit of her swollen eight-month belly, she knew something was wrong. Trying to hide her troubles from their untainted daughter, Sam quickly turned her head and wiped the lone tear that was already three quarters a way down her smooth mocha cheek.

Sensing her mother's somberness, Cadence gently grabbed her mother's glowing pregnant chin, as she so often did to hers, and looked her in the eyes and said with innocence and with all sincerity in her voice, "It's going to be okay, Mommy. I love you, and God loves me. So that means he loves you too, right, Mommy?" Samantha was shaken up by her daughter's observation, and nodding her head and hating those wet, salty entities falling from her eyes, she hugged her daughter and said, "Yes, baby, that is right."

It was at that very moment that she realized just how much her family meant to her, and the thought of losing them had her son doing cartwheels, as if to warn her of the destruction that would come if she let the devil destroy not only her marriage, but also her children. So with these thoughts and a heavily laden heart, she rose from the bed to go find her husband. Samantha walked to the door, grabbed the handle, but before she exited, something turned her to her daughter, and she said, "Caddy, no matter what happens, know that daddy and I love you, and always remember that God, like mommies, know how to take great care of his children." Cadence face lit up into a smile bright as summer, and Sam saw the silver lining and knew that better days were ahead, she just hoped they were nearby.

Sam left the room on a love mission, and in the most wifely, most loving, most girl-like voice, she called her husband. *Quincy, baby, I need to talk to you for a moment.* Samantha couldn't finish her thought because their doorbell rang. "Who could this be?" she said to Quincy, who had yielded to his name being called.

"Are you expecting anyone?"

"No, but it could be Daniel. I know he needs to take a load off after what happened today." Sam nodded in agreement and walked to the door, while Q walked back into their den.

Finally reaching the door, Samantha opened it to find herself greeted by a stranger.

"Hello, how may I help you?"

"Well, I'm not sure if you can help me, but I am looking for Quincy Tilt."

Astonished by this bold statement, she calmly asked this unwanted visitor, "May I ask who you are and what exactly is it that my husband can help you with?"

On the other side of the threshold stood a face of impatience, and then it spoke again and this time loudly. "Look, I need to see Quincy, so can you please go get him." This time, Sam said nothing; instead, she slammed the door so hard the wind from the door left her breathless. Catching her breath would have to come later because right now, she was about to catch a case. Just getting ready to head into the den, she heard her husband coming from around the corner, and he asked, "Sam, baby, who was that yelling at the door?"

Almost reflectively, she got in her husband's face and pushed his forehead with her index finger and said, "I do not know, but you better handle whoever it is because she sure as hell knows you." Not in the mood for another fight, another step backwards, not in the mood for another ten minutes full of regrettable words, he gently pushed Samantha aside and walked to see who was on the other side of the door.

After opening the door, he was standing face-to-face with the beautiful ghost of cupid's past. Had he been prepared, he would not have stood wide yet mouth open, yet not speaking, stunned by the figure that was before him. Samantha broke the silence and inquired of her husband, "So, Quincy, I see you do in fact know who she is"

"Yea, who am I?"

Quincy looked from his wife, to this stranger, and back to his wife, and back over the threshold and said to no one directly, "This is Melissa Nimadi, Cadence's biological mother."

9

STILL IN SHOCK of what just took place in his office, here in God's house, he could not help but wonder if everyone had simply lost their damn minds. Though the issue of Cheryl was still lingering, he had yet another major issue to deal with, and that was the mother of his church. Daniel found himself emerged with the burden of dealing with this task. See, it was this very same woman who claimed to be saved for nearly thirty-five years yet still promoted gossip. He found it ridiculous that she would cause such a mess and not see herself in the middle of it all. Yes, it was time. He was tired of her rumor spreading, ungodly slandering mouth, and he could no longer allow her to get away with it because she was elderly and because she had been faithful to the ministry for many years. However, he had to rethink the faithful part because being faithful to a building meant nothing. It was her faithfulness to God that he was beginning to question.

Suddenly, he realized that he had not taken a seat since Cheryl bragged in, and just as quickly, he realized that he was tired. He took a seat in his comfy brown leather executive chair, laid his head on his imported Italian hand-carved desk, and counted backwards from ten. Feeling his tension lessened slightly, he said aloud, "I need a break!" How could he do this for the rest of his life? As he sat there thinking, he felt the cool, comfortable, expensive heated leather chair beneath him. He also felt the sternness of his even more expensive desk, looked around his beautifully decorated suite, and sadly, it wasn't enough. He was preaching because he wanted to. He was preaching because he'd been called, right?

"Yes, I preach for God," he said so loudly that he startled himself. "Devil, you can't take that which is not yours. My joy, my peace, my sanity belong only to God, and therefore, you cannot take possession of it." Almost instantaneously, he felt the layers begin to fall, and he quietly asked the Lord for more patience, more love, and more power to give birth to the manifestation of Christ.

After thirty minutes of calming and self-motivating his mind with words of encouragement, he stood up with his head high, chest out, and decided that it was time for him to go home. Why he would choose to go there was even beyond him. After all, he had no wife, no kids. "Man, I ain't even got a dog." And that began to sink him deeper into what he just talked himself out of because now he didn't even know if he had a possibility with Cheryl. He was walking to the door when he heard voices coming from the sanctuary. "What now?" he said, obviously frustrated.

He turned and headed toward the connecting door, and though he needed to speak with her, Mother Hollister was the last person he wanted to see, but what better time than the present to ruffle some branches.

He stood in the doorway just over the threshold waiting for Mother Hollister to finish praying, and this made him laugh to himself. See, he found her kneeled position a joke because though her body was physically surrendered, in thirty-five years, it was obvious that her spirit had not conceded to Christ. While waiting on her to finish, he felt his iPhone vibrating, among all the ruckus he hadn't even felt or notice that it was ringing off the hook. He looked at his screen and noticed that he had eight missed calls from Quintin, but he was in no mood to talk and knew that he only wanted to know what happened in the meeting with Sister Lackey.

Turning his attention back to the sanctuary, he heard, "And, Lord, I ask that you touch the heart of your people so that they may see themselves and repent in order to turn from their ways so that they may see you one day." Daniel had heard enough before Mother Hollister could get *amen* good, and out he cleared his throat, motioned for her presence, and reentered his office. In her normal fashion, she walked in, and before he could say anything, she said, "Now I know why you want to see me, and before you get all mad, just know that what I did was for your own good. You see, Pastor Shepherd, the more people who know, the more people who can pray. That's what the great book says."

Though he tried very hard to retrain his frustration this woman was making, it was very difficult to, and before he realized it, a laugh had escaped his mouth. However, he knew he had to be stern, bluntly honest, and under the unction of the Holy Ghost.

"Mother Hollister, you can't honestly believe that you gossip out of good intentions rather than your own selfish needs." He found himself raising his voice and took a moment to gather himself before he continued. The room was silent. Daniel couldn't believe she had said nothing, but he welcomed the silence and took that time to pray. He asked God to disclose the root of Mother Hollister's unhappiness because surely, only a miserable person would intentionally hurt others and bring chaos. So he asked, "What's going on? What is it that is making you so angry? What is it that saddens you so much that you feel the need to be the Anne Bishop of this ministry? I mean, I want to know, I need to know because I care. I am your pastor, your overseer, and I want to help you." Looking into her aged yet graceful face, he saw something he'd never seen before—strong defiance. And at that moment, God revealed to him what the problem was, and he had to separate himself from the situation personally and exercise authority and bind the spirit that was holding this lady hostage for so long. Disrupting his train of thought, he heard, "Even if there was something wrong with me, if you think that I would tell you anything, think again! With all due respect, Pastor, you're the same person I caught nearly having sex in the house of God."

"You can't be serious?" Daniel asked her becoming irate all over again.

"Yes, I'm serious. Learn how to behave, and there won't be anything to spread, at least not about you. See, now I know that everyone can't be just and holy like me, but I mean with all due respect, Pastor, at least try."

Daniel had had it. He was done, and it was time he let her know who was in charge of this house. "Are you free from sin? I admit that I am not perfect, but I love the Lord, and I don't have anything to prove to you. I'll tell you another thing. The difference between you and I is that you fail to see yourself. You're judgmental, arrogant, and spiteful. You hurt people on purpose because you're a lonely and unhappy woman. You will stop the gossip, or I will remove you from the mother's board. After all, if you cannot follow, how can you lead? If that doesn't stop, you will leave this ministry. Please understand that I am serious, and as you've heard me say many times before, if you don't like the way I run my ministry, you are free to leave on your own freewill."

Mother Hollister couldn't believe he'd spoken to her in this manner, but the fight in her wouldn't let her concede to defeat. So she looked her pastor square in the eyes and asked with her eyes rolling and her neck turning in circles like she was involved in an exorcism, "Are you done yet?"

Pastor Shepherd hadn't the strength to answer, so he simply crossed his arms, placed him across his chest, and nodded. And with that, his head mother walked out the doors in his office without even the smallest good-bye. After his door had been slammed for the second time that evening, he leaned back in his chair and let out a sigh of frustration. He reached into the second drawer where his secret stash of Advil was stored and quickly washed down not two, but three of them with the glass of water that had managed to stay on his desk and not in his face. He began to feel his pants vibrate again and was bothered by the vibration of his cell phone. He was tempted to turn it off, but he looked at the caller ID anyways, and surprisingly, he saw Cheryl's name across his iPhone screen. However, he knew that was one call he definitely ignored. He simply was not ready to speak with her.

He rose, walked to his door, and said with his eyes averted to the hills, "Lord, your time is not our time, or your plans our plans, but while you worked it out on the cross, please, oh, please, work it out in my life."

10

"He's ignoring my calls. How dare him when he clearly is wrong here." Cheryl was livid yet, at the same time, filled with remorse that she acted in the way that she did. How can she get angry with him when she was harboring a secret of the past, which no doubt would stampede on her future? Though her past was a huge part of her future, she couldn't help the way she felt, She had broken the rules. She had fallen in love with Daniel, and he had to forgive her; he just had to. She still had not made it home because her car seemed to have a mind of its own after leaving Daniel. Her car, like her emotions, was out of control.

Having decided to go home, she was immobile by the storm of her tears. She pulled over off the road and gave into her unstable emotions. She wept because she knew she had to tell him everything. She wept because she knew in her heart that though he would forgive her, he would and could not forgive her. How could she tell him? Where would she start? What could she say to make him believe that her intentions were not to hurt him but to fix up a situation in her past? How could she tell him that she had sold her soul to what she had become to think of as the devil? Speaking of that devil, her phone rang. Looking at the ID, she dreaded answering but knew it would be in her best interest to do so anyways.

The voice on the other end said, "How is everything?"

"Fine, I guess. Look, I don't want to do this anymore. I think imma just tell him the truth." Cheryl knew those words were ones that held the weight of one-thousand-war vehicles heading into an authorized warzone. However, this, what Cheryl felt, was best not only for Daniel, but also for herself as well.

"You're going to do what!" the caller yelled into Cheryl's ear. "You're going to nothing of that sort. You gonna shut your mouth and do as you're told if you that location."

Though Cheryl had regretted the decision to make an arrangement with the devil, at that instance, she knew that the world she had worked so hard to build back up was all at once coming apart. However, she had to stick to her guns and speak her mind. "Look, he is too good of a man to do this to any longer. It's not right, and I made my decision, and you and I both have to live with it. However, I would rather lose him than to live with you holding my past over my head. I'm tired of playing these games. The game is over!"

"Lose him! Lose him! Ha! He ain't yours to lose, honey. As soon as he knows the truth about you, he gonna be on the first thing smoking back to Holyville. So shut up, do you hear me? Shut the hell up, and stick to the plan, or you'll regret it. I just need a little more time. I'm almost done." With that, the voice hung up, and Cheryl wept even louder than she had before. After an hour of feeling sorry for herself, she finally was calm enough to drive, and it was then that she decided she would visit her father. She wasn't ready to be alone. She just wasn't ready to face herself.

Cheryl had had a rough life growing up, and she did some things that she was not proud of, and that was the reason she was being held in bondage. "Lord, what am I going to do now?" she said through her tears. She then decided that God was still awesome and that because she had made decisions without consulting him, he was the only one who could turn her situation around and allow it to work in her favor.

Her father greeted her before she had a chance to knock on his door. At sixty-four years of age, she couldn't believe how awesome he looked. Though shrunken from years of wear and tear, he still stood six foot tall, had dark beautiful skin and very few wrinkles. He was also very active, which had him in fairly good shape. He had all his natural teeth and the biggest, deepest brown eyes you would ever see. To top it off, his salt and pepper hair, instead of making him look old, made him look distinguished and wise beyond his years. Overall, he was extremely attractive for his age.

"How are you, baby girl?"

"I'm cool, pops," she lied.

"What brings you by today?"

"I was just on my way home from church and thought I'd stop by. I'm still waiting on you to come." This made her think of Daniel.

Seeing the change in his daughter's face, he grabbed her hand and asked in all sincerity, "Sweetie, what's wrong?"

"Everything's okay, pops, just thinking about someone, that's all."

After catching up for another thirty minutes or so and declining a dinner invite, she finally decided to head home.

"Don't be a stranger, baby, and I promise I'll come to your church next Sunday."

"Okay, pops, sounds great."

"Love you."

"Love you too, Daddy."

The time she'd spent with her father was great. It had lifted her spirits and made her forget, at least for the moment, what she was going through. However, when she pulled up in her driveway, she couldn't forget because there, at her home, in her face was the constant reminder. There was Daniel.

11

Where was Daniel? Quincy had been trying to reach him for the past hour, and all he got was his voicemail. He needed to talk to his friend. Man, he needed to talk to his pastor because he didn't know what to do. However, after his failed attempts to reach Daniel and two angry women staring at each other, he knew he would have to handle this situation now before it got out of hand. Quincy decided to speak first, and the first words that naturally came out of his mouth was "Melissa, what are you doing here?" Without hesitation and boldly, Melissa said, "I came to see my daughter."

Sam jumped in before Quincy could answer and said, "Your daughter, your daughter, ha, don't worry yourself with the whereabouts of my daughter. You have some nerves. Your daughter? Just because your trifling behind, gave birth to her doesn't make her yours. I've been here since she was eight months old, and you think you can just waltz up to my house and demand to see my daughter. Where have you been for the last three years? Daughter! As far as I'm concerned, you have no daughter."

Realizing that his wife was becoming highly upset and too emotional especially being eight months pregnant, he had to calm her down. He stared at her, rubbing her swollen belly fiercely and breathing heavily. He feared she would go into premature labor and that he couldn't have, so he would have to choose his next words carefully. "Baby, why don't you go have a seat or go keep Cadence company while I handle this. You or my son doesn't need this stress right now."

"Hell, no, there is nothing to handle, Quincy. She needs to leave now!"

"Samantha! Baby, please let me handle this. Go, relax."

Though hesitant, she knew he was right because her baby's life depend on her being cool, so she turned and walked away. But for good measure, she turned and looked that woman square in the eyes and said, "Fine, I need to get back to my daughter anyways."

Unmoved by the last statement, Melissa turned her attention back to Quincy and said, "Q, I want my daughter!"

Finding himself sounding like his wife, he said, "Your daughter, you walked out on your daughter, and I told you that if you left, you couldn't come back. Now as my wife stated before, I think you should leave because you have no children that resides at this residence."

Melissa was irate. Though she knew she made a mistake, she still felt as though she was entitled to her daughter, and she couldn't believe he was treating her this way. After all, he did love her once, and she was sure if he would just hear her out, he would love her again, and they could be a family. However, she would have to deal with them later because she had come for her baby, and she would not be denied. Quincy was done with this conversation, and as he was about to slam the door, Melissa yelled, "I will take you to court."

Never being the one to back down from a threat, he stood his ground and told her, "Go ahead because that'll be the only way you'll ever see her again." And he slammed the door in her face. The next thing he heard were tires screeching as the mother of his child drove away.

Not a minute after the door closed, Samantha came out yelling and screaming. "Is she the reason you've been so cold, so distant?"

"Samantha, of course not. I've just had a lot on my mind, baby, that's all."

"Bull, Quincy, save it, okay. Because if you're up to your old tricks, I'll just take my children and leave. Is that what you want?"

That last comment infuriated him, but he understood and chose to ignore it. "No, that's not what I want, honey. I want my family. I love you, and I'm sorry you had to go through this today."

See, at that point, two things happened: the first, being that experience thought him that when a woman was upset and had a right to be, no matter what she said, the smart thing to do was to shut up and take the your right honey road; and second, he realized just how much he loved and needed her, and every doubt or insecurity he had faded, and he refused to let a woman who had deserted him and his daughter to cause him to lose his family.

Samantha was in tears, and because of all the yelling and screaming, Cadence had come out of her room, and she also was in tears. Samantha ran to her beautiful daughter and held her. She loved this child so much, and the thought of sharing her, the thought of losing her scared the life out of her, and she seriously would take her before she let that happen. At the sight of his wife and daughter in tears, he walked over and embraced them and allowed his wife to release all her stress unto his shoulder.

Even in the midst of his uncertainty, he realized that this is why it was best to follow God's plan because having children before marriage changed the equation, and this was the price he had to pay. However, he realized that the only way they would get through this storm was together.

12

Mother Hollister couldn't believe how that man had spoken to her. Since leaving the church, she drove home in silence, something she hadn't done for quite some time, though she would never let Pastor Shepherd know he had hit a weak spot. Was that it? Was she just not listening anymore? Driving back to her empty drafty home, she had no choice but to face herself and talk to God.

See, this time, there were no shouting, no music, and no friends on the other end of the phone. This time, she was alone, and for the first time in about fifteen years, she saw herself. She found her hands gripping the steering wheel tightly and felt the very thing she disdained. She felt tears forming in her eyes, and she hated her weakness. However, through her years of hypocrisy, she had read a few scriptures in her life and remembered that God hears the cries of his people and that if we seek after his righteousness and harden not our heart, then surely, the Lord, our God, will replenish us with strength and give us the desires of one's heart. So instead of denying the Holy Spirit, she opened her mouth and said, "Lord, I come before you humbled and completely surrendered unto you. It's been so long since I've spoken to you, and even longer since I've allowed you to speak. You see, Lord, I've been angry with so many people for all the wrong reasons when in all honesty, my anger is with you. I mean, I have not been blessed with children of my own, all my family is dead, and I've been coming home to a quiet, lonely house for far too long. You see, Lord." And like Jesus, she wept.

Wept at her dead spirit and like Lazarus, she needed Jesus to heal her body and raise her from her spiritual death. She just couldn't face the reality of her situation. The truth of the matter was that she was miserable, lonely, and let's face it—*Whose gonna want a cynical sixty-year-old woman?* This thought made her bawl. It made her shake. She didn't want to die all alone and unhappy like her mother. These thoughts made her unstable and irrational. She hadn't paid any attention to the fact that her epiphany had led to a river of thick, drowning tears.

Was she still driving? Where was she? It wasn't until her car swerved that she noticed her eyes had been closed. And when she opened them, all she saw was the tree, and everything after that went black.

13

CHERYL PULLED INTO her driveway, unsure of what was about to happen. "Lord, please not yet, just give me a little more time," she sighed, turned off her ignition, and exited her black on black Nissan Murano. She opened her door and swung her legs around and just sat there for a second, though it felt like an eternity. She exited and didn't dare to look the way of her pastor, at Daniel. Hell, she didn't know the line had been crossed, and she couldn't clearly define it anymore.

Meanwhile, Daniel watched her. He didn't know why he was there. He didn't know why he couldn't just let her go after that stunt she had pulled. He watched as Cheryl walked into her home without acknowledging his presence, and he said nothing as she quietly closed the door. Daniel got out of his Lincoln MKZ, and with unsure steps and unsure words on his tongue, he knocked on her door. He didn't know what he would say or what he would do, but one thing he just figured out was that he loved her and would try to work this out.

Between her car and her house, Cheryl had begun to cry. She was terribly afraid of losing him. See, in the midst of her assignment, she had lost control, and unfortunately, she loved him, though she wasn't supposed to. Daniel's knock jolted her back to the present, and she opened the door. She was beautiful to her, and she was beautiful to him. For a second, they stared at each other, allowing their silence to speak far better than their words could. For Daniel, what began as a friendship had developed into companionship; and for Cheryl, what began as an agreement with a third party evolved into a love so intense she thought she would die without it. In spite of a valiant effort, she could no longer hold them back, and the pain and fear she felt had made their way into the atmosphere as tears.

Daniel couldn't take it, he couldn't stand to see her pain. He wiped her tears away with the back of his large hands, and he kissed the spots where her tears had stained her face. And for Cheryl, it cleansed her spirit. And at that moment, nothing else mattered but the two of them.

"Daniel."

"Sssh. Cheryl, please don't say anything. Let's just forget about today. Let's forget about the past. Cheryl, I'm trying to build a future with you, but, baby, I'm begging you for once just be completely honest with me. I see that there is something holding you back from giving yourself to me completely. Tell me how you feel, tell me the past that is holding you captive."

"Daniel." God, how she loved to hear his name roll of her tongue and escape through her full lips. She loved this man with her very being, and because of that, she threw caution to the wind and decided to tell him the truth. "Daniel, I am completely engulfed in your reality. You make my senses come alive in ways I never thought possible. When I'm with you, I am superwoman. I've tried fighting this since the first time I shook your hand. I love you, and there is nothing, I mean, there isn't anything that will ever be able to change that." Cheryl was downright relieved. She was emancipated. In that instance, the truth had set her free. She was now ready to tell him about he r past. However, she realized that they were still standing on her doorstep, and she didn't want anybody in her business or put Daniel in a compromising position. So she motioned for him to step inside and take a seat. When entering, Daniel was still impressed on how he could walk into her home without notice, and it be well kept, and she did not have to tell him to hold on so that she could hide the dirty clothes, throw the dishes in the dishwasher, or air spray her bathroom. After coming inside, she sat on her deep red leather sofa and patted the seat next to her inviting him to sit next to her, though in reality, she needed that seat just as much as he did. Though he loved her, she realized that she was not only confiding in her *boyfriend* but that she would also be confiding in her spiritual counselor. And at that moment, she was going to back out but decided she would not be led by her fear, but instead, she would be led by her love.

There they were on her couch, and though silence was screaming, Daniel decided against speaking first, instead he waited on her to begin. Cheryl began to speak, but she wasn't facing him, and that was one thing Daniel wouldn't compromise on. She would have to face him because if they were to establish a meaningful relationship, there would be no shame, only transpierces. "Cheryl, please look at me. You don't have to be ashamed with me, no fear, I'm not judging you. I know I am your pastor, but I love you, and today, my sole purpose is to be your emotional pillar."

With that, Cheryl turned to him, and though still not apprehensive, she began her story. "Daniel, I want to tell you about my childhood after my father left. I want to tell you why my mother and I were estranged. I didn't tell you before because I thought you wouldn't be able to love someone with my experiences in life. There's just so much I gotta tell you, so much you may not forgive me for."

"Cheryl, who am I not to forgive? Surely, if God can forgive mankind of their past, then I can forgive you."

"Thank you, but you may not feel that way after everything is out in the open. Okay, my mother died from AIDS caused by sharing needles during her heroin addiction. My mom had started using about two weeks before Daddy left, and naturally, she got strung out when he finally left. Mom used all our money to feed her habit, which often led me to scrapping food from the garbage or wherever it was available, even if I had to steal it. One day, in order to settle a debt, her dealer wanted to see some girl on girl action from her. So my mother obliged with her own eight-year-old daughter. I guess that awakened something in her because it became a habit until I was eleven years old, then I ran away, and after the state investigated, I became their ward. I was moved from foster home almost twice a year because I had hella emotional issues, and nobody wanted to deal. It remained that way for about three years until my dad found me. By that time, I was fourteen years old. Once my dad found me, we bonded immediately and have been inseparable ever since. Naturally, I asked my father why he waited so long to come for me, and he said because my mother told him a drunk driver had killed me. To my knowledge between the time, I was taken, and I saw her again. She had had another baby, but the state had taken that baby as well. It was a little girl.

"When I was about twenty-four, I was in a committed three-year relationship, or so I thought until the nigga burned me with gonorrhea and chlamydia. Since that day, I have been both single and celebrant, that's been over seven years now. So you see, that's why I view sex and relationships the way I do because in my life, sex has always been used as a controlling mechanism. So I vowed that the next time I exchanged in the act, it would be on my own terms and when I was ready. That's why loving you is so scary because everyone I should have been able to trust has only used my body to harm me without a hint of remorse."

With tears streaming down both their faces and her trembling limbs, Daniel pulled her close and just held her fragile body and her frail hears. And for the first time in a long time outside of her dad, she felt peace in the arms of a man. Out of the silence from the darkness of her life, there they were bonding and becoming one. And with his chin rested on her head, Daniel softly whispered, "I love you."

Though Cheryl thought she saw love in his eyes when he looked at her, it felt awesome to hear him finally say it, especially after what she just revealed to him. However, in the back of her mind though, she knew she had made progress. She also knew that the biggest challenge was ahead and that she was just not ready to tell him.

They sat on the couch as she wrapped in his masculine arms, wrapped in her long thick legs, and she looked him in the eyes and said, "I love you too, Daniel."

Aroused by their intimacy and her words, he gently pulled her hair and filled her mouth with his kiss and his scent sent every muscle in Cheryl's body into shock, and she instantly felt her panties moisten. She felt his manhood press against her thigh. Remembering their last encounter, Daniel abruptly pulled away, no doubt trying to fight the temptation. "Please don't stop, Daniel, I want you." And with that, Daniel carried her into her spacious master bedroom. laid her on her pillow top king-sized bed and rested on top of her and with his eyes searched for her true emotions and it was there that he saw her frailty and for the first time he saw her completely vulnerable.

"Cheryl, you are an amazing woman, and your strength is undeniable. You have been a light in a personal life full of darkness." Cheryl felt a tear roll from her eyes, and this made her feel alive because she had been denying herself of all the love that Daniel was filling her with and she felt that it was time to let herself go. After those thoughts left her mind, the only thing left on it was him, and she grabbed Daniel by his collar and submerged herself in his kiss. Looking forward to the bulge that had formed between his thighs, she unbuckled his pants, and she seductively took her time sliding the belt from its loops and although she was fully clothed, Daniel nibbled on her breast, and he himself couldn't wait to become one with her

Cheryl pulled his shirt over his head and took a moment to appreciate the time he put into his body. She stood up and poked her butt out so that he could get a full view of her rear end, and she slid him slightly off the edge of the bed so that she could remove his pants and then went his briefs. Cheryl placed his manhood in her mouth, and at that moment, he was not her pastor, he was simply the man she loved. Daniel rested his head on her freshly washed pillow case and exhaled. See, he had forced himself to forget just how good being a man felt, and at this point in the game, he decided that God would simply have to deal with him later. He grabbed her head and gently gave her all of him.

Never being a selfish lover, Daniel stood her up and threw her on her bed and stated hungrily, "Now it's my turn." Daniel lifted her from in front of him and threw her unto the bed. He mounted her, and he roughly removed her shirt and took no time in between before her pants followed suit. Now she lay naked before him, and he had to admit that she had the most gorgeous body he had ever seen—every curve was beautiful to him. He glided his hand across her face and continued down the entire length of her body and taking extra time to palm her waiting love tunnel. He began by sucking on her breast and Cheryl let out a moan of pleasure. He then flicked his tongue across her navel, and without further ado, he dove into her nectar. Daniel decided that he'd had enough, and when he parted her lips, she shuddered. He took his time with her and made each stroke a well-thought out plan. He loved her like no other she'd ever known. He filled every inch of her being, and her body began to shudder. He flipped her over and took her from behind, she was amazing. After a few more strokes of love, his body began to shiver, and he exploded, releasing and leaving what could have been his child behind, and she quickly followed. As she lay in his strong arms, she knew that their lives would never be the same again, but that was what she hoped for. With Cheryl in his arms and his needs thoroughly fulfilled, and with their scent embedded into his nostrils, he fell asleep with a slight smile on his face.

14

Quincy slammed the door to the house he shared with his wife and daughter, slid down to the floor, and leaned; banged his head continuously on the nicely decorated door with a thud. He couldn't believe that this woman had the nerve to show up at his house five years later demanding his child. At that very moment, he realized that after all these years, she was the same selfish, inconsiderate woman she had been the day she walked out on them. With this realization, any uncertainty he had was gone, and he knew he couldn't and no longer love her. And in the same sense, he knew that his wife was nothing like her, and he was madly in love with her.

Speaking of which, he got up to go get his woman from the only place he knew she would be—with their daughter. He gently tapped on the door and let himself in, and what he saw filled his heart with joy yet, at the same time, with fear. As he watched his wife cradle their daughter and caress her curly black hair with tears rolling down her face, he knew that she was thinking that she could lose her baby. This time, the air between them was that with sadness and uncertainty. Samantha was the first to speak. "Where did she come from, Quincy? I don't know what I would do if I lost her. Please do something, baby." Samantha could control her emotions and began to shake uncontrollably, and Quincy rushed over, took their daughter from her mother, laid her in her princess tiara bed, grabbed his wife by the hand, and led her away from the room and did what he should have done a long time ago—he held her.

He allowed his wife to cry into his chest without repentance, and while she cried, he thanked God for restoration. He took a step back, and he noticed how she was glowing and just how beautiful she was with his son growing inside of her. He kissed her forehead, and she squeezed him so tightly, he thought he would pass out. She missed him, and that was his fault. He kissed his wife deeply, passionately, longingly, and freely. And in midkiss, he picked her up and carried her into their room and made sweet gently love to her, and when he was done, he kissed and rubbed her belly. He began to speak the Word of God in his son's life and proclaimed that he would be a stand up man for Christ and realized that God had in fact changed his very core.

15

Mother Hollister awakened to bright lights and white coats. When she opened her eyes, she looked up into the face of a middle-aged white man, and though she could see his lips moving, she could not hear his voice. Everything was moving in slow motion, and her life seemed to be playing as a PowerPoint slide show before her. She was going to die. With everything that she had in her, she prayed; however, she did not close her eyes in fear that she would not be able to open them again. The doctor must have been thinking the same thing because he urged her to keep her eyes open, and he begin clapping his hands and screaming her name. "Ms. Hollister, can you hear me?" he yelled, and this time, she could, and for that, she was grateful. He must have sensed that she could not respond verbally, so he instructed her to blink twice if she could in fact hear him, and she did.

"Ms. Hollister, we are taking you into surgery. You were in an accident, and we must perform surgery in order to save your leg. If you understand what I am saying, please blink twice." She did. "We found your identification on you at the accident scene and transported you to the nearest hospital. We couldn't find any next of kin information, but we did find your pastor's number in your purse, so we will be giving him a call once we stabilize you. Is that okay?" She blinked again. She was now in a cold room, full of metal and white, and they must had given her something because before she completed another thought, she was once again asleep.

16

DANIEL LAY IN the bed looking down upon a sleeping yet beautiful Cheryl. He traced her smooth arm of silk with his oversized fingertips and admired her beauty. He reminisced on the knowingness that had flowed between them and found that he was torn. He was torn between the preacher God had called him to be, but he was also torn by the love he had for this woman. Cheryl made him weak, and he had not yet figured out if that was a tick of the enemy or a gift from God. He had to admit though that if it led him into sin, then it had to be the devil because there was only two: right and wrong.

He was jolted back into reality when he felt the rise and fall of her voluptuous size D breast and became conscious that he was a pastor laying naked in the bed of one of his members, but she was more than that, and they smiled because they were breathing at the exact same time. He continued to think about their sexual encounter and how they were in fact animals because they were insatiable, and he filled her with his love three times in one night. And he understood that he simply had been backed up, and just thinking about it made his manhood tingle and eh could feel an erection forming. And he knew that he had to get up, roll over and out the bed, put on his clothes, and get out of her place because he knew that he would take her again if he did not.

Though his thoughts were that of a rational man, he did the most irrational thing that he could have done at that moment. He knew he should have just shaken her so hard till she caught a migraine and woke up. However, he decided that he would wake her up with a gently placed kiss right above her navel. Cheryl wiggled at his warmth and begin to guide his head down to her love place and happily obliged to do so. However, he was stopped because, man, he was being convicted by the Holy Spirit, so he unwillingly rose and propped himself up on one elbow and unpretentiously said, "We can't." And Cheryl, knowing not only his position but her secret as well, shook her head and said, "I'm sorry, you're right." Her humbleness excited him even more, and he began to stroke her face and gently massaged her hair, and she looked at him longingly and placed a trail of hisses from his well-sculpted chest to his beautiful mocha full lips.

It wasn't long before the sweet kiss elevated to heavy breathing, and Daniel had to stop himself. So he grabbed her by the arms and told her that it was in both of their best interest to get out of bed, get dressed, let him make her breakfast, and discuss what had happened between them and decide where they would go from there. She agreed.

Daniel found himself in Cheryl's kitchen making ham and cheese omelets and laughing to himself because this woman must have really put it on for him to be cooking. As they were about to begin talking about the future of their relationship, Daniel's cell phone rang, and though he didn't recognize the number, he answered.

17

"Hello, I'm trying to reach a Mr. Shepherd. Is this Daniel Shepherd?" the deep inquiring voice sound on the other end of the phone asked.

"Yes, this is Pastor Shepherd. How can I help you?"

"Well, we are calling because we found your number in the purse of Bertha Hollister, and we need you to come down to Saint Peterson Community Hospital."

"Oh, my God, is she going to be okay?"

"Yes, she'll be fine, Mr. Shepherd, please do calm down. She is a little banged up and has a broken shoulder, but she'll be just fine in a few weeks. We just thought she would like to see a familiar face when she wakes up. Are you her next of kin?"

"No, sir, she has no family. But I'm her pastor, and I'll be there shortly."

"Okay, thank you, Mr. Shepherd."

"No, thank you, Doctor."

Daniel hung up the phone, turned to Cheryl who was already watching him intensely, and said, "We have to go to the hospital. Mother Hollister has been in an accident." Without hesitation, Cheryl flew into the room and threw on something a little more decent, grabbed Daniel's jacket and shoes, and dashed back into the living room. "Thank you, baby," Daniel said, as Cheryl handed him his things.

"Is she okay, Daniel?"

"Yes, she's fine. But I'm pretty sure she's afraid, so it's my job to see that she is okay."

"Okay, love, then let's go."

Cheryl and Daniel turned to each other and in unison asked, "My car or yours?" They both shared a laugh and for a moment forgot about Mother Hollister and stared into each other's soul. And though their connection was undeniable, Daniel still saw it—a blemish on her soul—but what was it? Guess he hadn't fallen too far from grace last night because his spirit of discernment was still intact, but he couldn't, for the life of him, figure out what it was.

"We gotta talk and soon okay?"

"I know."

"Okay, now let's go."

They hopped in Cheryl's Murano and headed toward the hospital. While in the car, Daniel held out his hand, and Cheryl instinctively placed hers on top, and almost subconsciously, Daniel began to pray. "Heavenly Father, I come to you humbled, stained. And with a spirit of repentance, I ask that you forgive us for our sins as we lift up not only the body of Christ, but also the heavy heart of Mother Hollister to you. We ask that you heal broken bones and broken hearts. We pray that you restore her to complete health, and we thank you in advance for the continuing abundance of love, race, and more importantly, mercy that you have even though we are undeserving, amen."

"I love you, Cheryl," Daniel said almost to himself. And then he turned to her and said, "I've been thinking about going to see my father. I can't preach forgiveness and not completely forgive him for taking my mother. The sad part is I lost my father that day too, and I miss him greatly. I miss him." Cheryl turned to take a glimpse at him and saw the lone tear that had escaped his beautiful eyes, and she took her palm and washed it away. Daniel couldn't take his eyes off her and was amazed when she kissed the spot where his tear once laid. "I love you too so much." Cheryl decided they had about ten minutes before they reached the hospital, and she would spend those minutes explaining and begging for his forgiveness. "Baby, when I—," in midsentence, her phone rang, and when you sell your soul to the devil, he can show up whenever he liked. She knew she had to answer because those were the rules of engagement. "Hello," Cheryl said visibly irritated. "Look," said the voice. "Keep your hands off him, slut, and stick to the rules. I'll be back in about two weeks so get it together." Click! Unbeknownst to Cheryl, Daniel was staring at her with a strange look on his face. And before she could say anything, Daniel asked, "Who was that?"

"Oh, that was just a friend of mine," Cheryl lied.

However, Daniel could have sworn he heard a voice so familiar that it sent chills up his spine, but it couldn't be. So he shook it off, just as they pulled up to the hospital.

18

DANIEL AND CHERYL went through the tall automatic doors of the emergency room and went to the receptionist in order to find out what room Mother Hollister was in. When they walked into the cold dark room, they treaded lightly in an attempt not to wake her, but in her usual form, that didn't work. She woke and smiled when she saw Daniel. Cheryl was cautious because of what had gone on with her and Daniel and how Mother Hollister reacted. "How are you feeling, Bertha?" he said softly and genuinely concerned. "Pastor, I'm all right, just a little scared and banged up. I can't believe you even came after the way I behaved. I'm sorry, and that Cheryl is a good girl." Daniel was speechless, and all he could do was thank God. He motioned for Cheryl to come. She did and greeted Mother Hollister with a kiss on the cheek, and she graciously accepted. "So glad you're okay. We prayed for you."

"Thanks, it's always needed. Pastor, I want you to know that I've changed and that I am here for you if you need me, and to let you know that I am proud of you."

As Daniel sat with Cheryl, he began to think about how gracious God truly was. He most certainly was a God of a second chance. Daniel was thanking God because after his wife died, he didn't think he would find love again. But looking over at Cheryl, he knew he had, and he was thankful. However, she was holding something from him, and before this year was out, she would tell him. Interrupting Cheryl's conversation was the ringing of her phone. She excused herself. In an attempt to make small talk, Daniel asked Mother Hollister if she needed home to call her insurance and if she needed any help financially. "Oh no, that's quite all right. You have enough to deal with. Are you ready for your sermon tomorrow?"

"Not even close, but I have some serious talking to do with the Lord tonight, so I'll be ready.

"Well, Mother, I don't know where Cheryl is but imma gone head and let you rest, but if you need anything, don't hesitate to call me."

"Okay, I won't and tell Cheryl that I said good-bye."

With that, Daniel walked out of the room, into the hall to see Cheryl on the phone. "I'm ready to go," He said shortly and bluntly. Well, what's wrong with u Cheryl asked, and he answered "that phone gone get you in trouble, so I suggest you

Fix whatever issue you have with it and do so fast.

Daniel was checking his voicemail because with all that was going on, Daniel realized he had missed Quincy's calls, and he made a mental note to call him back as soon as he got off the line. The first voicemail was from Quincy, however, the other was a bit strange. Someone blew a kiss into the receiver and then just sat there until the time allotted on the recorder. What was going on? First, he could have sworn he knew the voice on the other end of Cheryl's line; now this voicemail, and he was almost certain Cheryl had a secret bigger than Texas. And though he had fallen short, he was still tapped into the Holy Spirit, and he was discerning that something wasn't right and that Cheryl knew what that was. Daniel let out a sigh of slight frustration but gathered himself. He would not jump to conclusions. He would control his emotions, seek God, and wait. He disconnected from his voicemail and dialed Quincy's number. He picked up after one ring.

"Man, where the—man, where have you been? D, you supposed to be here for me, man. I need to talk to you."

"I'm sorry, Q. I just forgot to call you back. A lot has happened on my end as well in the last five days. What's up? Who you need man—your pastor or your friend?"

"I need 'em both, man!" Quincy explained to Daniel everything, and Daniel had empathy for his friend.

After listening, he finally spoke, "As your friend, man, I know it must be tough for you. I'm glad you realize that Melissa ain't no good and will never be, and I'll give you my lawyer's number. He handled my paperwork after Traci's death. Now as your pastor, I'm here to tell you that this too shall pass, for the Bible declares that all things work for the good of those who believe in God. Love your wife and only your wife. No one of anything should ever come between the two of you. You hear me, Quincy? Q, man, do you hear me?"

"Yea, I hear ya, man. Sam is a wreck. I'm so worried about her, but I do believe God is going to work it out for us, but enough of that. You sound drained. Are you okay? What's going on?"

"Man, Ma Hollister was in an accident, so I had to go up there, and this was after she showed out again about Cheryl. Oh, and speaking of which, she barraged into my office when I was in a meeting with Sister Lackey acting stupid."

"Naw, man."

"Yes, man, that ain't the end, let me finish. I go to her to get an explanation, and we slept together, man. I don't know how I allowed that to happen."

"D, we both know what you did was wrong, but you, as human, ask God to forgive you and move on. But on a fleshly note, how was it? Cuz Ms. Gooding sho is thick." They both shared a laugh and Daniel interjected. "Shut up, don't talk about her like that. But, man, it was amazing."

"Hold on, D. You, you love her, don't you? I can hear it all in your voice."

"Yeah, I love her, but she hiding something man. I just know it." Daniel decided not to mention the voice he thought he heard because Quincy would just tell him he was crazy. "Well, man, let me go. I was just calling you back. I'm home now, and I gotta get my message together for tomorrow's sermon. See the two of you in my office."

"No, man, Daniel, we just talked about this."

"I have to pray on it, and I need to speak with you and Sam, got it?"

"Yes, Pastor Shepherd."

"Thank you, Deacon Tilt."

Daniel walked into his modest home. And now that he was alone, away from the craziness of his week, he could feel the chastisement of Christ. And he knew that he was on and popping because in a battle between God, it's funny how he always manages to win. Daniel opened his Bible, and as he did, he felt liberated from the filth of his weekend. He praised God because he still knew him. He praised God all because he was God. It didn't take long for God to speak to him, and though this would be a hard one to preach, he headed to obey. Daniel was shaking his head and said to himself, "You've got this." However, when he looked at the title again, he wasn't one hundred percent positive about that. He asked again, "Lord, are you sure?" And he heard a small, still unmovable voice say, "Yes, title your message, I too am a sinner!"

19

Daniel sat in the pulpit, unsure of how he would deliver this message, unsure of what he would say, how he would feel. He was scared, but he knew he needed to deliver the Word that God had given him not only for himself but also for his congregation as well. So for the first time in the long time, he allowed his praise team to usher Christ into his spirit, and he was led to the alter as he internalized that we served an amazing God that specialized in forgiveness. And he decided, at that moment, that those very words would be the very way he opened his sermon. He scanned the crowd and didn't see Cheryl and was secretly hoping she missed this particular Sunday. However, that prayer would be unanswered because she walked in with a man who Daniel assumed was her father, and he knew this would be one of the hardest Sundays he had in a while.

"The book of 1 John 1:9 says that if we should confess our sins, God is faithful and will forgive us from our sins and cleanse us. Now that is an awesome God. And today, I want you to know that I'm just as grateful for that forgiveness as you are." Daniel spoke truth. He spoke the gospel. He spoke freedom, and he was amazed at how a message that he so deeply dreaded actual was exactly what he needed. In his usual fashion, he greeted his attendees as they exited the sanctuary. And this time, he wouldn't take forever because before service, he had gotten a text from Quincy, and he was anxious to go see his godson. He wondered if Cheryl wanted to go with him but thought that she might have plans since she was with her father. He reminded himself to text her and ask.

"Hello, Pastor Shepherd."

"Cheryl, how are you, dear?"

"I'm well, thanks for asking. I want to introduce you to my father."

"Hello, sir, how are you doing?"

"I'm well, thank you. You preached a great Word today. It just reminded me of how great God really is because trust me, we all need forgiving," he said this with such conviction, as he looked at Cheryl. It made Daniel wonder just what he was talking about. "Pastor, I've heard great things about you. It's a pleasure. Is that right? Well, that's a blessing. It was good meeting you."

"Cheryl, Sam had the baby. You wanna go with me to see him, unless you and your father have plans already."

"Um, no, we don't actually. So you can pick me up in about an hour and a half."

"Sounds good. See you then. It was great meeting you, sir."

"And you as well, son."

Daniel arrived at Cheryl's house and blew the horn, and when she came out, Daniel thought she looked like Christmas morning in Denver—stunning. They greeted with a kiss and began their fifteen-minute drive to the hospital. Daniel had stopped by the store to get the baby a few things and couldn't believe how excited he was to meet this little boy. Cheryl couldn't help but to think that the last time they were together at a hospital, this same hospital, the entrance felt cold, icy, and scary. But this time, entering the hospital on Daniel's arm felt warm, inviting, and full of hope.

When they entered the room, all they felt was love, and it was beautiful. Daniel went to Samantha. "Hey, beautiful, how you feeling?"

"Good, thanks for coming. Hello, Cheryl, how are you?"

"I'm well, thank you. Congratulations, honey."

"Q, my man, congratulations, man," Daniel said, as he hugged Q. And Q whispered in his ear, "No wonder it took you so long."

"Yeah, man, had to get my lady. Now let me hold my godson." Daniel sat in the chair and just looked at baby Quincy, and he began to feel something that couldn't be explained. He loved this little boy beyond life, and he could only imagine how much he would one day love his own children. This made him think of Traci. He still couldn't fully believe that he was gone from him. The plane landed in the Atlantic, and her body was never recovered, and he honestly thought that was the reason closure was so difficult with him. She was his everything. He had loved his wife. Sure, there were times when he just wasn't sure if she was ready to be in ministry, and that left him uncertain about their future. But she genuinely loved him, and that was enough for him at the moment. He was looking forward to having babies and raising them as a family. He must have been so wrapped in his thoughts because when he looked up from baby Q, Cheryl was standing at his shoulder, asking him if he was okay.

"Yes, I'm fine, got lost in this kid for a second there."

"Well, can I hold him, silly?"

"Of course, love."

Looking at Cheryl hold and play with Quincy gave Daniel all the fuel he needed and no longer did he regret their night of lovemaking because he wanted to make things official with her and marry this woman. After all, he did love her, and he was ready to be a husband again and, most definitely, a father. They spent hours in the hospital just talking, laughing, and celebrating life with their friends, but it was time to go. In the car, the air was filled with everything they were feeling, yet refusing to say, Daniel decided to be the first to speak. "Cheryl, I want you all to myself. I love you." Cheryl was left speechless. She looked at the man she loved, and just as they pulled into her home, she burst into tears. This secret was killing her. "Cheryl, baby, what's wrong?"

"Daniel, I have to go. I just have to go. I love you so much, but we can't be together. I'm sorry."

Daniel sat in the car flabbergasted, not sure what just happened. But this time, he would not brush it aside. She was going to tell him what was going on, and she would do it now, or she would lose him forever.

Daniel was banging on the door like a mad man, yet she refused to open the door. He just didn't understand what she was keeping from him. "Cheryl, please let me in. Baby, I need you, I love you. Please open the door."

"Daniel, please just go away. I'm not worth it."

"Cheryl, please, whatever it is, don't just leave me, not like this."

Cheryl could no longer take it, so she opened the door and just walked away. Daniel came into the living room and sat beside the silhouette of the woman he loved. There was no sound, just air thick like the early morning fog. He couldn't believe he begged her, but he had grown fond of her, and he had to fight. Cheryl's tears burned her cheeks, and she searched her soul to try to find the words to say to him, but she couldn't. There was no way that he would forgive her for what she had allowed to take place. She decided that she would just hold him tonight and that tomorrow morning, she would disappear. Cheryl grabbed his head and rested it just above her breasts, and she rubbed his head. Just as she was about to plant a kiss on the top of his head, she heard her phone vibrate and knew that the devil was very well aware of the game they had been playing and how it was turning out.

Cheryl just let the phone ring, and the light from the phone illuminated the room, yet somehow, it pulled them both back into darkness. He wrapped his arms around her waist and continued to rest in her bosom, and he couldn't help but let a tear escape his eyes because he knew that he might have lost the only woman he had loved since his wife. Sadly, Cheryl was just about drowning in her own tears, and when she felt his tear run down the spilt in her chest, she sighed and could no longer hold back. So she cried—cried for the love that she was losing, cried for the trust she had broken, cried for the man who she would hurt, cried for her heart. And Daniel allowed her to cleanse her indiscretion and felt the weight of her tears absorb in the roots of his hair. Yet through all his uncertainty, he held her without ceasing, without condition, without hesitancy. He held her like Christ holds on to hope that we will get it right one day, and he hoped that she would too.

There they sat with life between them, and through her tears, she whispered "I love you," and she meant it. But she also knew what she had to do, and it was best for the both of them. "Daniel, there are things you don't know about me. Things that will probably make you hate me because they make me hate myself. However, I can no longer be held hostage by my past, the things I let take place in my present, and I can only hope that you somehow find a way to allow me to be in your future. When I reunited with my father, he hadn't quite gotten out of his lifestyle. And one night, our house was broken into, and this man was trying to rape me. I screamed, yelled, cried out for help, but nobody came. I managed to get away, and I ran into my father's room. And when he burst through the door, I shot him! I still remember the sound of the gun going off and the echo from his body hitting the floor. What was I supposed to do? I wasn't about to let anybody, I mean, anybody else take advantage of me. I was terrified, too afraid to call the police, so I waited until my father got home. And once he came home, my father helped me cover it up. And that's why we moved here to get a new start—to move on from the past.

"When I moved here, I didn't look back and had asked God for forgiveness, gave him my life, and I moved on. I know what I did was wrong, but I couldn't go to jail, and no one would believe my story." Daniel sat up looking at Cheryl in disbelief. He couldn't believe what she had just revealed to him. He looked at her, and she was just a fraction of the woman he had fallen in love with. Her hair was a bit unkempt, her eyes were puffy because of all the tears, and she was a murderer. He attempted to say something, but she stopped him. "Wait, before you say anything, there's more. Remember when I shared with you that I had a sister I didn't know? Well, somehow, she found out about my secret and where we had buried the body. She found me, and she is now blackmailing me in order not to tell my secret. See, a few weeks before I met you, she gave me an ultimatum. I was to join the church, keep women away from you, or else she would tell the authorities my secret. So I agreed."

Daniel finally spoke. "Wait a minute, you're telling me that all this was some sort of game to you? That it was all a lie that you used me? After knowing what I been through, how could you do this to me?" Daniel asked through tears that were as heavy as sandbags. "I'm sorry," Cheryl wept. "I didn't know how awesome you were. I didn't think I would fall in love with you. I tried, I tried to call it off, I tried to tell you. But every time I tried, she would throw it up in my face, and I always caved. Please don't, please don't leave, at least not before I tell you everything."

"There couldn't possibly more to tell."

"It's about my sister. I didn't know at the time that she was—" Before Cheryl could finish the sentence, her front door swung open, and there, just above the threshold, stood the devil—the ghost of the past—and Daniel couldn't believe his eyes. And as he tried to speak, no words would escape, instead, they formed balls in the middle of his throat, and he passed out.

20

Quincy and Samantha returned home to find that it had been destroyed. Quincy instructed his wife to stay at the door while he looked around to see if the perpetrators were still inside. Quincy couldn't believe how they had pulled every picture off the wall, every dish out the cabinet. They had even broken Quintin's bed, everything except the things with Cadence in it. And when he went into Cadence's room and saw it was still completely intact, he realized that this was no accident. He looked around more and noticed a piece of paper sticking out from underneath Cadence's pillow. The statement was simple: "I will get my daughter." Quincy tried to hide his worry, but his wife saw it all over his face, and he was forced to tell her. "We have to call the police, and we have to make sure we cover all our bases, so we have to go back to the lawyer. She must know she has no case, or she wouldn't have done this. She has always been irresponsible but never has she been stupid. I don't want you to worry, Samantha, I'll take care of this. I'm going to have someone come in to help clean this up. I'll go get the baby a new bed, but I just need you to take care of our children."

Quincy left the house with a few things on his mind. First, he would get his son a bed, but more importantly, he would find Melissa, and he would tell her one more time to stay away from his home and his daughter. After stopping by their old stomping grounds and riding around for hours without even a single sign of Melissa, Quincy decided to go home and be with his family. He tried calling Daniel, but there was no answer, so he didn't try anymore. Quincy walked into his home and was pleased that it was clean and pretty much back to normal, except for the fact that it was quiet, in fact, it was too quiet.

"Sam, baby, Cadence."

Quincy could feel his heart taking the plunge from his chest to his stomach, and he just didn't like the fact that he'd been gone for hours, and his daughter hadn't greeted him at the door. Quincy searched the entire home, and he chose to check Cadence's room last because he wasn't prepared for living without his family. As he pushed opened the door, he saw Melissa on the bed with Cadence sitting in between her legs crying, and when he turned and saw his wife gagged and she and his newborn son tied up, he almost lost it. Melissa stared at him with malice in her eyes and venom in her voice and spat. "Hold on, big boy, you may wanna think about what happens next cause I'm holding the trunks right now."

"I'm going to kill you bitch." As soon as he got the last word out, Melissa flashed a 9mm gun and pointed it toward Samantha and Quinton and simply stated, "If I go, we all go, except for my beautiful baby girl here."

"Daddy, I'm scared, Daddy, please." At the sound of his daughter's pleas, he buckled under the weight and gravity of this, and all he could do was fall to his knees and began to cry. Samantha couldn't bear to witness him like this, and she too felt tears running down her cheeks, and all she wanted to do was hold her husband and comfort her daughter.

"Don't cry now, fool. I came here, I tried to do it the right way. But instead of just giving me my baby, you wanted to be nasty and keep her from me."

"You left! You walked out on her how many years ago, and you just show up and expect me to hand you my daughter! Hell, no! Look at what you're doing, and you wonder why. You have always been so damn selfish. Let my family go, leave now, and we can just forget about all this."

"In case you haven't figured it out by now, I'm not leaving here without her."

Melissa was focused on Cadence, and Quincy used that to lunge and tackle her. She landed on her back, and before he knew it, he was on top of her. Their daughter was screaming, and he was killing her by strangulation. He tried to pull back. He tried to listen to the voice in his head telling him to stop. But the more Cadence bawled—when he looked over his shoulder and saw his son and wife bound and his wife gagged—he squeezed tighter, and he found himself smiling as he faced lost color. Melissa had always been a fighter, and she had no plans on dying at least not tonight. So she found some way to kick Quincy in his life givers, and he lifted up, fell back, and yelled. And with that, Cadence couldn't take it anymore, and Melissa was infuriated that he was going to kill her. So she pulled her gun, pointed it, and with one last breath, she looked him dead in the eyes and said, "I told she is going with me!"

Samantha could only look on what was taking place, and with her son strapped to her chest, she was sure he would feel her agony and die. So she tried to maintain her cool, but she was finding it hard to see with the amount of tears flowing from her eyes and the sound of Quintin's wailing. She could only pray that, somehow, someway, God stepped in.

As the same was thinking this, she heard Quincy say, "If you want her, you're going to have to kill me." Melissa replied, "Your wish is my command." She fired two shots, and in the spilt second, it took the bullets to hit Quincy. Cadence yelled "Daddy" and jumped in front of him.

21

DANIEL AWOKE TO the sound of screaming, and as he adjusted his eyes, what he thought could only be a dream reminded him that what he had seen was real.

"Cheryl, how is this possible?"

"Daniel, baby, I'm sorry."

Daniel scanned the room until he found what he was looking for, and all he could do was bawl.

"Don't cry, baby, aren't you happy to see me? Didn't you miss me? I'm alive. Aren't you happy?"

"Traci? What? How? What's going on? You're dead, at least you're supposed to be. I don't understand."

Daniel picked himself up and sat on the couch trying to make sense of everything that was going on. He didn't understand how she could be alive, and if she was, why she would want him to believe she was dead. He looked from Cheryl to Traci, then from Traci to Cheryl, and at that moment, he hated them both. His heart was telling him one thing, but his head was screaming something more. He wanted to run to Traci, hug her, kiss her, love her, but he just couldn't understand why if she was alive all this time and had allowed him to experience such agony.

"How is this possible? Why didn't, how could you, why would you? Answer me, Traci!"

"Baby, listen, I missed you so much, but I just had to get my mind together. I wanted to be perfect for you, and I just needed space to breathe, to live a little bit out from under the church spotlight. So I went to the airport but never got on the plane, and I had every intention on calling you, but when the plane crashed, I took advantage of the opportunity. I know it was wrong, but we can fix it, right? The most important thing is that I'm alive, right, baby? I know if anybody understands the strain of this lifestyle, you do."

"The only thing I understand is that you are a lying, heartless woman, and I didn't know you at all. What's funny is that you should've stayed where you were because you're dead to me, and this is one death you will never come back from."

Traci couldn't believe her ears, and she looked over at Cheryl who was standing in the corner and spat. "This is your fault. Nobody told you to go and sleep with him, you slut!"

"My fault? I didn't even want to do this, but no, you insisted, and your evil spirit had to have your cake and eat it too. You were so sure that he'd forgive you. Guess the laugh is on us because neither one of us will have him."

"Yea, but I'll get you! I know your little secret. I know where the body is buried, and as promised, I will tell the cops everything!"

Daniel was sick to his stomach with Traci, and he wanted her to leave his life forever. He, at that moment, no longer loved her.

"I'd hold off on calling the police," he said. "I'm sure the police would be interested in knowing about the fraud you had to commit to pull this off. I'm sure they would also want to know if you've paid taxes, collected on any life-insurance policies, and committed any other countless crimes—I'm sure that comes along with faking your own death. So I suggest you go back to where the hell you came from because I want no parts of you and anything you could possibly have to offer." With that, Daniel walked to the door, opened it, and waited for Traci to leave. He felt nothing.

"Baby, I'm sorry. I'm ready now. I realized how much I love you and how much I need you. Please don't do this. How can you not forgive me, but can forgive her?"

Daniel didn't blink, he never looked her way. He simply widened her escape route and said, "Good-bye, Traci, and have a great life." With that, Traci kissed him on his cheek and walked out, and they never saw her again.

Daniel closed the door, and he just stood there. He didn't move, didn't blink, and didn't speak, just stood there and stared at Cheryl. He knew she was hiding something, but

God knows he didn't know it was this big. He wanted to run and comfort her because part of him could understand why she did what she chose to do. She must have been so very scared, but then the other side was filled with rage. He had shared with her so much of him, yet that still wasn't enough for her. After all, she couldn't even be honest with him.

"You should've just been honest with me, but instead, you have ruined everything. I loved, love you, and I thought we were building something great only to find that you were behind enemy lines."

"Daniel, I'm so sorry, you have to believe me. I wanted to tell you so many times, but the fear of not only myself but also my father spending the rest of my life in jail was greater than that feeling. I'm so sorry I hurt you, and if you give me the chance, I promise, I promise I won't ever hurt you again. Just don't leave me."

"How can I trust you? How can I look at you the same? Was any of it real, or was it all a part of the act?"

"No, it was real. I just didn't expect for you to love me back. I'm sorry. Please don't leave. You can't."

"Why can't I? Give me one good reason why I should stay."

"Because I love you, I need you. We need you. I'm pregnant!"

22

SAMANTHA COULDN'T SCREAM, but her eyes told the story of a mother and wife horrified at what just took place. Tears fell as she watched both her daughter and her husband motionless on the floor. All she could see was blood, and she held her son so tight that he began to cry. Melissa ran over to Cadence's motionless body, and her eyes went from her to Quincy, from Quincy to Samantha. What had she done? She removed the tape from Samantha's mouth and paced the room.

"Listen here, okay. If you say something, I'll kill your son. Do you hear me? I'll kill your son. Now I gotta get out of here. I know y'all loaded, so where is the money?"

"In the bank! Let me loose so I can get help for my husband and daughter, please!"

"Your daughter? She's my daughter. I was just young, scared. I was confused, but I've always loved them. He just couldn't let it go, he has always been emotional. He just couldn't allow me to see her and now look, look what I've done. I killed the only two people I've ever loved! I was hoping, just hoping he forgave me and left you, and we could've been a family again. This is all your fault, and you know what they say, the best witness is a dead witness. So I'll tell you what I'll do. I'll kill you, and you took my daughter, so I'll take your son."

Melissa grabbed Quintin, laid him on the bed, and then she pointed the gun at Samantha. Samantha heard a loud noise, and a gunshot followed.

"Mrs. Tilt, are you okay?"

Samantha opened her eyes to see police officers in the room, paramedics performing CPR on her husband and daughter, Quintin hollering on the bed, and she glanced over and saw Melissa glossy eyed in the corner, looking directly at Quincy and Cadence. She realized that there is nothing on the earth more powerful than love or even the perception of it, and we had to be careful who we allowed not only into our home but also into our hearts as well. Once she was freed, she ran to her family, and as she held her son, she cried and prayed that her daughter and husband would be okay.

23

Daniel finally found the wooden floors that were slick under his weight, and all of a sudden, the oak door felt like a ton of bricks on his back. *How did he allow this to happen? What was he supposed to do now? He loved her, but she had betrayed him in the worst way.* However, she was carrying his baby, and that was someone he couldn't turn his back on. So even if it meant he'd have to deal with her, he would because his child would know what a father was. Then there was the pastor thing. He wanted to please God. And since he loved her anyways, maybe he should marry her. That would have been okay just hours ago, but now, how could he do so? At this moment, what would their foundation be? He had a lot of thinking to do because he also had to remember he had a church to run, and surely, he would be ran out of town like a witch in Salem once the congregation found out that he was having a baby out of wedlock. He had really gotten himself into something bigger than him, so he would do what he does best and pray before making any type of decision because that was the best thing to do.

Cheryl sat looking at him, wondering what he was thinking. She wished she knew the words to ease his burden, to alleviate his pain, but she didn't. She hated to be the cause of his discomfort, and she needed him to know that she loved him and that she would have never done this if she knew it would lead to all this. He was her soul mate, and she needed him to forgive her and take her back. She needed him. They needed him. She was afraid to speak first because she thought it would run him off, so she would sit and wait for him to process everything that happened to him tonight. She would wait as long as it took because the fact that he was still there meant to her that there was hope. So she decided to cling to it, and while they were sitting, she was praying—praying for forgiveness, praying for provision, praying that God would give her another chance and renew what she had destroyed.

"Cheryl, I need time to think, okay? I need time to figure out what it is that I am going to do, regardless if I choose to be with you or not. I just want you to know that I will be there for my baby I love you, and I want you to know that so my decision, if it is to not be with you, won't be because I didn't love you. It's just—"

The phone rang, and they looked at each other in complete fear, afraid that it was Traci or the police. Daniel picked up his phone and saw Sam's number and let out a sigh of relief.

"Hey, Sam, what's up?"

Cheryl watched as Daniel's eyes spread wide in shock, and she swore she saw the color drain from his face, so she ran over to him.

"Sam, where is Quintin? Where are you? Okay, I'm on my way."

Once Sam was safely off the phone, Daniel went numb. Did she just say what he thought she said? How? Why? He needed them to be okay. His hands were shaking uncontrollably, and his phone fell, and he caved. It was all too much. His wife was alive, his girlfriend was having his baby, and now he had just found out that his best friend and goddaughter had been shot. He looked up at Cheryl and saw genuine concern in her eyes. He saw love and a woman wanting to be there for him not because she was trying to get back but because she really cared, and it was at that moment he forgave her. He knew it would not be an easy journey back, but he knew it was one he wanted to take with her. He could no longer hold back his tears behind a makeshift dam built from eyelid, and he fell into her arms and released his frustrations. And she, she allowed him to do so.

"Daniel, baby, what's wrong?"

"Sam, Quincy, Cadence, please just get me to the hospital, please."

With that, not another word was spoken. She grabbed her coat, purse, and keys, and Daniel was already waiting outside by the car. Cheryl didn't know what had happened, but by the look on Daniel's face, she knew it was bad, and she had to get him where he needed to be and be whatever he needed her to be in order to save her family.

24

THEY ARRIVED TO the hospital, and Daniel found Sam in the room with Quincy, who was still not awake, and he hugged her. Cadence was in surgery, and Quintin was hanging from Sam's arms. She looked exhausted, famished, and terrified. Quintin needed to be fed. He was tired, cranky, and Sam simply didn't have the energy to feed him.

"Samantha, baby, why don't you give the baby to Cheryl."

Samantha snapped and yelled, "No! No! No! No one can touch my baby. I'm his mother. He needs to be with me."

Daniel realized that it wasn't them who she was lashing out at, but instead at the situation. However, Daniel needed her to be logical, and he needed to know exactly what happened and what was going on with his best friend and his goddaughter.

"Sam, it's me. It's Daniel and Cheryl. We are here to help in whatever way you need us. Sam, it's me. I love you, I would never hurt you or the children. Come on, give Cheryl the baby and allow her to take care of him, and I'll be by your side. She won't leave the room with him. I promise."

Daniel motioned for Cheryl to come over, and she made her way back to Sam, gave her a hug, and got baby Quintin. She called for the nurse, and when the nurse came, she explained the situation. That Quintin had nothing to eat, no diapers, and if they could please grab some from the maternity ward so that she could care for him. Since Daniel had promised Cheryl wouldn't leave the room, they had to wait until the nurse came back. So Daniel took that time to find out exactly what was going on. He couldn't believe that Melissa had done this. Sure sometimes, she was a little looney, but he never thought she'd hurt anyone. Quincy had been shot once in the stomach and hadn't come through, yet he was expected to be okay since the bullet missed the organs. Cadence had been in surgery for a little over an hour now as they were removing the bullet. He just prayed that everything would work out, but he knew not the plans of God, so he was trying not to question him. And though they say that the birth of a new life often signifies the ending of another, he sure hoped it wasn't one of their lives that would equalize everything.

Finally, the nurse brought some things for the baby including a whole package of bottles, wipes, and diapers. And Daniel watched Cheryl as she cared for the baby, and he couldn't believe she was carrying his child. However, he was confident that she would be a great mother, and for that, he was grateful. After a while of waiting for the surgery to be finished, a doctor finally came in. He asked if it was okay if he spoke around us and began giving Sam the update.

"Mrs. Tilt, the bullet was lodged in your daughter's lungs, and we were able to remove the bullet. However, upon removing the bullet, her lungs collapsed. She was just too weak. We tried everything possible, but I am so sorry to have to tell you that Cadence didn't make it out of the operating room."

The howl that came from Samantha was the saddest thing Daniel had ever heard, and though he was sobbing, he knew he had to be there for her. He ran over to her and got there just in time to keep her from hitting the floor. He couldn't believe what the doctor had said, and everyone, including Cheryl, was crying. He was angry, so angry with God. How could he allow this to happen? Why? He just didn't understand. He tried to find peace in knowing that God was too wise to make a mistake. However, seeing Samantha in so much pain and knowing that when Quincy woke up he would be devastated, he couldn't wrap his head around trying to understand what God was doing in this case. All he could do was hold Sam. Other than that, he didn't know what to do to console her. That's it. There was nothing to do to console a mother who had just lost her child.

Sam unwrapped herself from Daniel's arms and walked zombielike over to Cheryl and got her son, and she held him like her life depended on it. She held him and refused to let him go. She lay in the bed with her husband and her baby, and she wept quietly. And Daniel felt completely helpless. Cheryl was in the corner holding her stomach, not wanting to imagine how Samantha was feeling at the time, and Daniel rushed over to console her, he didn't even want her to think like that. He touched her stomach and embraced her, and they both cried for their friends. Sam and Daniel went to see Cadence and said their good-byes, and Daniel was hurt that his friend would not be able to say good-bye to his only daughter.

After being back and forth to the hospital for three days, Daniel and Cheryl thought it be best if they had professionals clean the place as they knew it would be far too difficult for either one of them, and having Samantha do so was out of the question. They went by the house to see the damage in order to know what exactly needed to be done, and they were not all ready for the scene inside of Cadence's room. The stench of blood was heavy, and knowing that some of it was hers was very emotional and once giving instructions, they left. On the way to the car, Daniel got a call from Samantha that Quincy was awake, and she needed him to tell him because she didn't know how. Neither did he, but he could only pray that God provide the words and the strength he would need to comfort his friend.

They arrived at the hospital unsure and feeling ill prepared, but it had to be done, and with God, they would get through this tough period. Sam hadn't buried Cadence yet, as she was trying to wait and see if Quincy would awake so that he could say good-bye. Upon entering the room, he saw his friend smile weakly and was happy to see that he was holding Quintin. He went over to his friend and gave him a huge hug and fought back tears the whole time. Daniel decided to waste no time, as no time would ever be the right time to tell him that his daughter was dead at the hands of her mother. He instructed Cheryl to get Quintin from his father, and he started the first word of the hardest sentences of his life. Daniel's voice was shaking and weak, as he went to answer Quincy's repeated inquires about his daughter's whereabouts.

"Q, man, Cadence was shot, and she had to have surgery. And her lungs collapsed, and I'm sorry, man, she didn't make it. I'm so sorry, man."

Quincy couldn't believe what he just heard and yelled, "Yo, D, don't play like that. Where's my baby? Where's my daughter? Go get my baby! Please, man, go get my baby, please!"

He looked at his wife hoping she would dispute what was just said, but she didn't, and he knew it was real when he saw her on the floor bawling, and then the rain came from his eyes and spilled onto his handsome face. Daniel comforted his friend, and Cheryl comforted Quincy's wife, and baby Quintin was in the midst of it all. After what felt like an eternity, Q spoke.

"How long have I been out, D?"

"Three days, man."

"Have y'all buried my baby?"

"No, man, we were putting it off waiting on you."

"I need to see her. Where is my baby?"

"She's still here."

"Take me to her."

"Of course."

Samantha rose to go with him, but Quincy instructed her to stay with their son and reassured her he would be okay, and he and Daniel went downstairs to allow him to say his farewells to his little girl. Once there, Quincy lost complete control and held her body and refused to let it go. After a while, Daniel convinced him to let her go, and he sat there for an hour and held his friend. And though it was tough for him, there was no place else he'd rather be, and he thanked God for giving him the strength to calm the beast.

Two days later, Quincy was released, a day after they held a private funeral with just the four of them and Sam's and Quincy's parents, and they laid Cadence to rest. Quincy and Sam thanked them for everything and walked to their front door. Somehow, Q's parents had convinced them to let them watch the baby for a while, and they were ready to walk into their home for the first time since that horrific day. Daniel offered to stay, but they declined, and he reassured them to not hesitate if they needed anything, and he and Cheryl went on their way.

Walking into the house was strange. A house that was once filled with laughter, and the smell of food was now cold. And even though it had been cleaned, well, it smelled of death. While Quincy was doing everything to avoid the room, Sam went directly to it, grabbed her daughter's favorite doll, held it close to her chest, lay on her double bed, and cried again. She missed her so much. Quincy finally entered the room, and he got one of her shirts. He joined his wife, and they cried together and knew their lives would never be the same without their princess. Neither of them moved for two days, and when they finally did, they packed their clothes, walked out of the home they shared with their daughter, and never stepped foot in it again. A week later, the house was on the market, and they were living with Quincy's parents until the house was sold.

Though it would be a long path, they relied on the love of God and the love they shared for one another and showered their young prince with love and were taking all the time they needed to heal and cried out to God, and he comforted them. They were thankful to still have Quintin, and at 3months old, he was the sweetest redemption song for Mr. and Mrs. Tilt.

25

CHERYL AND DANIEL entered their home and decided that the past was in the past and that life was too short to hang on to it. He was glad Traci was gone and the fact that they hadn't heard from her. He couldn't focus on that he had a child on the way, and he had to do right with the woman he loved and by God. He went into his room and came out with a box, a small wooden one, with a custom embroidered covering. He sat Cheryl on the couch and took her hand and said, "I forgive you, and I love you. I know that our road to trust and happiness will be a journey, but with God, everything is possible. I don't want my child to grow up in a home without me. I love you so very much, and I thank you for being by not only my side but also my friends' as well. You're a good woman, and I am not asking you to marry me only because you're carrying my child but because I love the Lord, and I want to please him, and I know if we both forgive ourselves and continue to put him first that he will honor this commitment and show himself awesome in our lives. Cheryl, it's already an honor to have you as the mother of my child, but I'd be just as honored if you would be my wife. Will you marry me?"

Cheryl couldn't believe how lucky she was, and she was so thankful she hadn't lost him. She looked at him with all sincerity, and she said to him, "Yes, of course, I'll marry you."

Daniel was honestly happy and overjoyed that she had accepted his proposal. He put his hand on her belly, began to pray, and they both couldn't wait to see their bundle of joy. And Daniel knew he had some work to do to get back in the Lord's grace, but he was more than willing to do whatever that took. He looked at his wife to be and said, "Hi, my name is Pastor Daniel Shepherd, and I will be an unwed father in nine months."